DOROTHY SUMMERS

ADVENTURE SERIES

DOROTHY SUMMERS

Mystery of the Blue Dragon

REDWRITER

REDWRITER

This book is a work of fiction. Reference to real people, events, establishments, organizations, or locales, are intended only to provide a sense of authenticity, and are used fictitiously. All other characters, and all incidents and dialogue, are drawn from the author's imagination and are not to be construed as real.

FIRST EDITION

Designed by REDWRITER

Library of Congress Cataloging-in-Publication Data has been applied for.

ISBN 978-1-7358826-2-8

One's value is weighed by their impact on others, determined by action, and driven by creed.

REDWRITER

PORT OF IMAGINATION

Issue 1

San Francisco, 1933. Such a forward time. The city has come such a long way since its birth during the outlaw era of the gold rush. Architecture, fashion, music. Art is at the cusp of progressive change and San Francisco is thriving with it. Although hope lies ahead for a brighter future, progress is often met with the unyielding human nature to resist change. This resistance has caused many people adversity on their path to contribute to society. None more than the person at the center of this tale, Dorothy Summers.

If anyone can relate to the widest array of the melting pot of humanity who have called San Francisco home, it would be Dorothy Summers. Dorothy is a third-generation Chinese immigrant, a realized ideal of the American dream. Just because she may be the poster child for the ideal equal society, the innate sins of humanity often creep in to delay the rise of tomorrow. Her father was an artist at the *San Francisco Chronicle*, where he met Dorothy's mother working in the mail room. You see, Dorothy doesn't just come from a blended cultural background. Her family background mirrors the diversity of San Francisco.

Her father is white, and her mother is Chinese. If you know anything about genetics or science, you will understand that the mix of races can lead to some of the best genetic outcomes. When our genes are created, the best genes are often cherry-picked from the basket of our parents. The more different our parents are, the wider selection we have for our genes to select stronger building blocks. Dorothy was built with some of the strongest seen yet. However, genes do not make someone great; the choices they make and the character they build do, and she is undoubtedly one of the most fierce and inspiring human beings you will ever get to know. We must first join her on her journey. The journey that made the world known to the woman we call Dorothy Summers.

Before we begin or go any further, I must implore you to grab your softest blanket, your favorite snack, and nestle up in the coziest corner of your home. This story is an adventure, that will set sail from the port of your imagination, and into the world of Dorothy Summers. You must curl up tight and dive in deep. The twists and turns to come will rock you in and out of your world and into hers. Now, you have exactly one minute and thirty-four seconds to grab your necessities before we flip this page and begin our journey into Dorothy Summers and the Mystery of the Blue Dragon.

SAN FRANCISCO CHRONICLE

Issue 2

Dorothy awoke from the short sleep she always seemed to have. She lifted her hand to her forehead to wipe the sweat that had built up during the night. The room was poorly lit, as the light of the rising sun had not yet reached her window in the skinny alleyway of her Chinatown apartment. Dorothy rose out of bed to stumble over to her window to shut it. The wind of the night never traveled through her window, but that never stopped her from leaving it open. You can never expect to receive good fortune if you close the door, or in this case window, to its path. Just because you haven't received good fortune in the past doesn't mean that you won't receive it in the future.

Not much time is spent getting ready. As a mixed Chinese-American in 1933 San Francisco, there's not much you can do to your appearance to change the way people look at you. For this reason, Dorothy didn't spend much time trying to change herself to please others' expectations of her. She was somewhat tom-boyish in the sense of fashion, but she did not sacrifice her femininity with her choice of comfort. She was a woman at her core but dressed unlike one most of her time.

Her outfit started with medium brown twill men's trousers with a wide cut leg that covered most of her small worn out leather oxford shoes. The waist of the pants was singed in tight against her abdomen. Dorothy was skinnier than the average woman, which meant that she did not have the coveted body plastered on the front covers of *Vogue* magazine. It wasn't like being skinny was a choice for Dorothy, as finding enough food to eat as the daughter of a starving artist is a feat in itself. Her family barley survived the Great Depression as it was. Climbing up the wardrobe you would find a loose-fitting delicate, white cream blouse tucked tightly at the waist into her trousers. The extra fabric of her blouse helped keep her pants from falling as she made her walks to work.

Finally, the hair. What you would think to be a bird's nest from lying down in the sweaty hot pillow of Summer nights, was more like a thick healthy drape of black hair that shined with blue glimmers as it was worked up into a bloom of the current women's fashion on top of her head. After readying herself for the day, Dorothy would make her way down the wooden steps of her apartment into the living room and kitchen, which doubled as her parent's bedroom. Her father would awaken upon hearing the creeks in the wood sound off in a rhythm as Dorothy would scurry down them with a spring in her step.

"Good morning, my beautiful masterpiece!", said her father. Dorothy's dad considered her to be his best work of art yet.

"Morning, Dad", said Dorothy endearingly.

"Off to work, are we?" the Dad conspicuously muttered.

"As always." Dorothy returned with a tone of sarcasm.

After the morning routine of greeting her father's use of humor to connect with her, Dorothy grabbed her camera and threw it around her neck as if it was as an essential an accessory as a string of pearls are to an heiress. Next, she grabbed her pad of papers and a chewed-up short pencil and stuffed it into her left pants pocket as she opened the door with her right hand.

"See you for dinner." Dorothy called out as she shut the door to the apartment behind her.

Dorothy gave herself forty minutes for what would normally take twenty-one minutes to walk. She liked to eavesdrop on conversations as she strolled slowly along the sidewalk to work. There was always a part of her that hoped to hear some headline-making gossip about a story not yet discovered. Dorothy had always dreamed of working at the *Chronicle* like her parents, but as a barrier-breaking investigative journalist. Dorothy grew up rummaging through her father's sketches at home pretending like she was a journalist on a hunt for a juicy story. She would often get carried away from her eavesdropping and into her daydreams as she meandered her way to 901 Mission Street.

HONK-HONK-HOOONK! The car horn of a Ford Model A startled Dorothy out of her daydream quick enough for her to realize that she had wondered off the sidewalk and into the street before the vehicle came crashing into her. Dorothy quickly jolted back up onto the sidewalk as the driver sped furiously by with a look of blame in his eyes as he glared at Dorothy.

Lee, who owned the meat shop in front of the incident, called out to Dorothy as he was hanging the daily duck from his shop's window, "That was a close call!".

"I know," said Dorothy, "Just a little caught up in my thoughts today."

"Well you better wake up before you end up like this duck here," instructed Lee.

"I'll take note," Dorothy said as she looked both ways before making a cross to the other side of the street.

Not long after almost getting run over in the street, Dorothy came up to the newly built *San Francisco Chronicle* newspaper's headquarter building. The building stood firm with a stout gothic styled façade and was crowned with twin clocks upon its corner tower at the entrance. Dorothy walked around to the side entrance, where she made her way swiftly to the mail room, making sure to not be seen. She wasn't one for calling attention to herself unless it served a purpose.

As Dorothy stepped into the mail room Ying, her coworker and friend, was across the table lifting the first bag of mail onto the table.

"You're late."

"Well, you could say I had a good excuse.", Dorothy debated.

"There isn't an excuse I can think of that would work for a Chinese girl...Why don't you put that camera up and help me sort this mail."

Dorothy grabbed the strap of her camera from around her neck and placed it on the table in the corner of the room.

"I don't see why you bring that camera to work every day. It can't help you sort the mail any faster," claimed Ying.

"No, but I can't expect to become a journalist one day if I never have a camera to capture the next headline-grabbing story," exclaimed Dorothy.

"Journalist?" scoffed Ying. "If they ever allow a mixed Chinese immigrant woman to become a journalist, please tell me. Because that'll be the day, I quit this job and become the queen of California."

Dorothy, not fazed by the doubt Ying had about her dreams, let the comments pass over her like a short breeze over the top of her head.

Dorothy began sorting through the pile of mail stacked up on her side of the table. Instead of taking the first one on the top, Dorothy always peeled through the layers to find the one with the highest prospects of containing something scandalous. Then there it was, the corner of a red stamp peeking out from a hole in the pile. Dorothy picked the letter out of the bunch like a bird hunting for the morning worm. It was from Shanghai and had the word "Urgent" in mandarin stamped in red across the front.

Eager to find out what could be so urgent, Dorothy ripped through the envelop to find a handwritten letter on the back of what looked like an autumn yellow cloth from a robe. She began to read through the letter with anticipation for her big break.

> *"To the one who is reading this. You don't know me, but I have asked that the universe would deliver this letter to a kind and strong spirit. One capable of exposing the evil actions of lost souls. The Tong Gang has captured my brothers and a far more important prisoner. I ask that you do whatever you can to stop their shipment of the Blue Dragon to the port of San Francisco. The natural spirit of the world and the creatures that belong to it depend on you."*

"Blue Dragon? Tong Gang?" whispers Dorothy under her breath.

"What was that?" asked Ying.

"I just found my ticket to the show with the editor." Dorothy responded.

"Please don't tell me you're thinking about going upstairs to try to talk to Mr. Henry again?" Ying asked.

"This time it's different." Dorothy said with a tone of confidence.

Dorothy folded the cloth letter and stuffed it back into the envelope. She gripped the edges firmly as she nervously made her way from the mail room to the writers' floor. This was a wide-open space full of desks and journalists, all white men who were now staring at Dorothy, who had arrived two hours earlier than usual. Dorothy paid no attention to the befuddled looks of the men in the room. Most of them were still too young to have a proper shave, but the aroma of the room was that of overindulgent aftershave and a haze of morning cigarettes.

After a slight pause after turning to stare down the path between the writers' desks to the editor's room on the other side, Dorothy began to walk towards Mr. Henry's office door. With each step her head raised a little higher as her confidence began to climb. Halfway there, one of the older more veteran journalists piped up to say, "What? Did you forget about all the other mail?" The other men began to chuckle. It did not phase her one bit. Seventeen more steps and she was there.

Dorothy stared at the opaque textured glass with the words "Arthur Henry – Chief Editor" painted at Dorothy's eye level. She raised her left hand in a fist to knock on the walnut trim of the door, that held the glass pane in place. The room went silent as everyone waited to hear what Mr. Henry's response would be.

"Come in!" Arthur shouted.

Eager to get the gaze of the men off her, Dorothy quickly opened the door and stepped into Mr. Henry's office. She heard the tapping of typewriters begin to chatter a few seconds after closing the door.

Arthur's head was buried in a review of some draft columns, when Dorothy entered.

"What is it now, Dorothy?" Arthur complained without looking up to see who had stepped into his office.

"How did you know it was me?" Dorothy asked.

"You don't smell like aftershave or cigarettes, which means you had to be a woman. And there is only one woman in this entire building who would have the guts to step into my office. So, what complaint or pitch have you deemed important enough to interrupt both of our jobs this morning?" said Arthur firmly and with a hint of annoyance.

Dorothy cleared her throat to regain her self-assurance. "An urgent letter came in this morning from Shanghai. It describes, what I believe to be a drug smuggling operation right here in San Francisco. The Tong Gang is involved. I believe this could be tomorrow's headline story and thought you would be interested." Dorothy explained.

Arthur's interest seemed piqued. "Let me see that letter." Dorothy handed over the letter as Arthur leaned up in his seat to grab it from her. He took the cloth out of the envelope and looked it over. Arthur began to laugh.

"What's so funny?", Dorothy asked.

"Little honey, this is why you should leave the real work to us men. I can't run this story. The source is a dopey-brained fool," Arthur stated as he threw the piece of cloth into his wastebasket underneath his desk.

"What if I chased the story down myself to investigate the source's claim? I could do it after hours, and you wouldn't have to pay me any extra," Dorothy offered.

"Of course, I wouldn't pay you extra. Do what you want outside of here, but I'm paying you to sort mail, not investigate it. Either way, I won't print what you find. A story about dragons is better suited for a magazine like your crazy uncle's down in Chinatown. Not for the *San Francisco Chronicle*, the news king of the West," bellowed Arthur.

Dorothy's anger started boiling up along her brow line. She went to grab the envelope off of Arthur's desk before he had a chance to throw it away too. She turned to leave his office. "Oh, and Dorothy, I suggest you stick to the mail room. If I catch you up here again, you're fired. You understand?". Dorothy didn't even give him the satisfaction of an answer. She stepped out of the office and walked down the sea of eyes of all the journalists who were turned around in their seats to see the damage Mr. Henry had caused. The look on their faces made Dorothy even angrier. She could see what they were thinking. They wore their thoughts on the expression of their faces like make-up. It was a look of *That'll teach her to stay in her place.*

When Dorothy got back to the mail room, Ying didn't even bother to utter, "I told you so." She could see that Dorothy had had enough and didn't want to poke the bear. The rest of the day dragged out longer than usual for Dorothy.

As clock-out time approached, Dorothy went to grab her camera off the corner table. What she once looked at as a symbol of hope, Dorothy now looked down upon as a dream that would no longer be possible. A tear started to form in her eyes as she lifted the strap around her neck. She quickly realized and sucked it back in so that it wouldn't fall down her cheek. She had had enough humiliation for one day.

Later that night, Dorothy sat on the edge of her bed going over the events of the day, while turning her camera over in her hand.

"Dorothy, dinner's ready!", shouted her mom from downstairs. Dorothy went downstairs more lethargic than normal. Her dad noticed this.

"Hey dumplin', I want to show you something I've been working on."

Dorothy amused her dad by following him over to his easel at the end of his bed, which was partly covered by a dirty cloth.

"You ready?" he asked.

"Yep," Dorothy said plainly.

Dorothy's dad went to peel pack the cloth from his easel to reveal a half-finished portrait of Dorothy smiling with her camera around her neck.

"Isn't it beautiful?"

"I wouldn't use those words exactly," claimed Dorothy.

"What happened today to put your spirits in such a blue mood?" he asked.

Her mom butted in, "You two can talk all about it around the dinner table."

Next to the stove top that doubled as a fireplace were two vegetable crates stacked on top of each other with a wooden board on top. Around this makeshift dining table were three short stools. Placed in the center was a pot of cabbage and potato broth soup. All three of the Summers gathered around the table as Father poured a bowl for everyone. He filled Dorothy's bowl with more potatoes than his. He would always claim it was due to the luck of the scoop, but Dorothy always knew he was trying to give her more food. She knew her Dad loved them and was always trying his best to take care of them. The warmth of his love was enough for her to break down the walls of her insecurity long enough to tell them about her day with Mr. Henry at the *Chronicle*.

After divulging the details of her day, she finally stopped to take a breath. Her father's soup had gone cold. He wanted to make sure he listened well, so he hadn't touched it while she talked.

"Well it sounds like your boss is blind to the talent staring him in the face.", her father said. "Although he may have had one thing right. If he doesn't print your story, I know your uncle will."

"Uncle? The only thing about Uncle that he got right is that he's crazy," Dorothy replied defensively.

"What some see as crazy now, others might come to find ingenious later," her dad rebutted.

"I appreciate what you're trying to do, Dad, but working for Uncle isn't what I had in mind," Dorothy stated.

"Well just remember to keep it as an option, if your plans change."

Dorothy retired to her bedroom for the night after dinner. She took a bath in a tin tub just big enough to sit in with her legs pulled to her chest. They would change the water out once a week. It wasn't enough to get her clean, but it did keep the layer of dirt and soot on her skin at bay, so it wasn't noticeable.

After cleaning up, Dorothy laid back in her bed. This time she did not open her window before laying down. As she laid back trying to go to sleep, she thought to herself, *What now?* Her dream of becoming a journalist was squashed and her family depended on the money her job brought in. She didn't know if she could face going back to the *Chronicle* knowing that the only thing that awaited her there was a mail room. Then again, her options as a woman were limited as it was anyway. Dorothy's worries carried her late into the night, giving her less sleep than usual.

WANG SHU'S MONSTER MAGAZINE

Issue 3

It was the next morning. Dorothy made it to the *Chronicle* earlier than usual. She hadn't taken her time to listen to the street gossip on the way to work today. All hope wasn't lost yet; she still had her camera hung around her neck as she entered the side door. Maybe Dorothy hadn't given up. She still had a window, her camera lens, slightly open to allow good fortune to pass through.

As Dorothy stepped into the mail room, Ying looked at Dorothy with a surprised look on her face.

"Why do you look so surprised to see me? Did you think yesterday defeated me?" Dorothy asked Ying.

"I thought they would have stopped you at the front door to tell you," Ying said in confusion.

"Tell me what?", Dorothy asked with some nervousness.

"You better go talk to Mr. Henry," said Ying.

Dorothy went up to the writer's room. Except this time, the men weren't in a joking mood. Instead, they pretended as if they didn't even see her standing at the entrance. The lack of attention created an awkward silence about the place. Dorothy tried to swallow the lump in her throat as she approached Mr. Henry's door. She raised her hand to knock. This time softer than the last.

"Come in," Mr. Henry called with a brashness toned with pleasure.

Dorothy entered Mr. Henry's room. "You asked for me?" Dorothy questioned.

"Yes, it's about yesterday." Mr. Henry began to explain, "You see, it takes a lot of hard work from a lot of brilliant men's minds to keep this paper successful. After yesterday's stunt, I got to thinking. I can't have my hard-working men out there continue to be interrupted in their efforts by a woman down in the mail room. And all because she still hasn't learned to know her place in this world. I really admire your gumption and childlike imagination of being capable of being a journalist someday. I truly do. But this is the real world we live in here, and that's just not possible. So, I'm afraid yesterday was your last day. You can go downstairs to collect your last payment from Edith."

The words rolled off Arthur Henry's lips with such ease. They were followed by a grin with wickedness camouflaged on the corners. The last time she had seen someone smile like that was when the boy in her apartment smiled as he crushed the robin eggs from the nest on her window, when she was a little girl. There is no other way to explain it, other than a certain type of evil had crawled into Mr. Henry's heart and rotted it black. Dorothy knew there was no arguing with a man like that. She turned to step out of his office. Just before Dorothy left, Mr. Henry decided to get one more comment in, as if he were addicted to seeing Dorothy's misery.

"Don't worry. A beautiful girl like you won't be out of work long in this city. All you need is some proper clothes and some make-up, and I'd might even choose to be your first customer."

Dorothy could feel Mr. Henry's gritty little eyes looking her up and down from behind. She took one more step past the threshold of the door, and slammed it shut so hard that the glass from the door shattered to the floor. "Art and Chief" were the only letters that remained. Then without looking back she said in the calmest voice, "Maybe one of your brilliant men will know how to fix that for you," before walking out and down to collect her payment from Edith.

Something was different about Dorothy the second she slammed that door. There was a fire inside of her that had been stoked by the vile words of Mr. Henry. The last bit of hope she was holding onto bloomed into a whole forest of aspiration. *No more*, Dorothy thought. She wasn't going to leave her fate in the hands of a pompous old man and his old-fashioned beliefs. This day was not going to end with her going home, head hung low. Dorothy was going to be heard and her dreams realized. Starting with the mystery of the blue dragon. *But where to start? Who would give her a shot? Who would help her?* Then she remembered her father's words about keeping an open mind to her uncle's magazine.

As Dorothy stepped out onto the sidewalk from the *Chronicle* building, she felt the weight of her steps lighten. It was as if she were leaving a prison and had left her shackles behind for a new future.

The first step in this new future included finding her uncle's magazine. She hadn't visited her uncle since she was just a little girl. Her mother had held a thirty-year-old grudge with her brother, ever since he used their parent's money to chase fake monster folklore around the globe. Dorothy's mother would always claim that their family would be in better conditions, if he had given the Summers some of the money to invest in a proper apartment. Dorothy's grandparents may have given her mom some of the money, if she hadn't fallen for Dorothy's dad, a white man.

As Dorothy took her next step, good fortune finally started flowing her direction. Dorothy nearly tripped and fell over a stack of telephone directories just delivered outside the *Chronicle*. She bent down to pick one up and flipped to the back of the book, to the W's. Her finger slid down the page like a penguin on an iceberg, before stopping right on it. "Wang Shu's Monster Magazine." There it was, and not too far from her apartment in Chinatown. Dorothy ripped the page from the directory and stuffed it in her pocket along with the envelope from Shanghai and headed out towards her uncle's business.

The smell of sweet pastries began filling the air in front of Dorothy. She traded off looking at the address on the page from the directory and back up at the numbers on the sides of the buildings. Eventually she found herself standing in front of an almond cookie shop with the same address as her uncle's magazine business. A little confused, the newly emboldened Dorothy stepped right through into the shop to ask the owner, if they knew where Wang Shu's Monster Magazine was. The owner reassured her that she was in the right place and said that they rent the upstairs space to Wang Shu.

"Would you mind, if I went up to see him? I'm his niece," Dorothy explained.

"Of course, I'm sure he'll be happy to see you. He doesn't have many visitors pass through here."

Dorothy squeezed by the tightly-packed bakery shop floor. It was packed to the ceiling with all kinds of sweet and savory treats. In the back was a red tattered curtain. Behind it was a steep and narrow staircase that led up to a landing with a green wooden door. It read "Wang Shu's Monster Magazine" in gold letters. Dorothy breathed out a long breath before knocking. *KNOCK-KNOCK-KNOCK*. "Door's open!". The yell came from the weak, crackly voice of an old man inside.

Dorothy opened the door to find a room the size of the shop downstairs. It was packed full of stock magazine papers, cans of used ink, an old industrial printer, and an old man sitting on a stool at a table near the window. He was tapping away at his typewriter. Underneath him was a twin mattress curled up on the ends against the legs of the table he was at. All Dorothy could see was the back of an old man hunched over his typewriter. "Uncle Shu, it's Dorothy," she announced.

Uncle Shu sat up straight to reveal the back of his head. His gray hair was sticking in all kinds of directions like a wacky circus clown. As he turned around to see her, he lifted a set of round glasses to his face so as to see her.

"Dorothy, it is you! Oh my, how long has it been?"

"About seventeen years," Dorothy claimed.

Without a moment for pause, Shu asked "Is that so. How's your mom, my little sister doing?"

"She's doing well. Still taking care of my dad," she replied.

"So what set of fates has bestowed this visit with my little niece upon me?"

"It's kind of a long story. But on the short, I was fired from my job, and I had a story I wanted to ask you to print," she explained.

"Oh my, oh my, one's poor fortune has turned to my good fortune. Tell me all about this story," her uncle requested.

Dorothy then pulled the creased envelope from her pocket and handed it to Shu before explaining what she had read on the cloth. After explaining what was written and how her old boss had thrown it in trash, she explained her theory of what it could mean.

"The note mentioned the Tong Gang, who are notorious for smuggling drugs through Chinatown. I believe this Blue Dragon they are speaking of is a new drug set to hit the ports of San Francisco Bay soon."

Shu begins scratching the side of his head. "And what is the story you would like for me to print?" he asked.

"The note on the cloth. Hopefully it would stir up some interest to inspire someone to keep following the trail," she said.

"Hmm. Uh-hmm. Yes, I won't print it," Shu said as he leaned back in his stool, folding his arms as he awaited her reaction.

"You won't print it? Why? Because it isn't about a real dragon? Your stories are all fake and hardly anyone buys your magazines. Why does it matter to you what you print in your magazine?" she whined.

Shu raised his top eyelid of his left eye to see when she was ready to listen. Then Shu began laughing like an infant being tickled in its crib. "And who says my stories on the monsters of this world are fake? Believe me when I say that the creatures mentioned in the ancient fables are no farther from the truth than the very nose on your face. Just because you've never seen it, doesn't mean it's not there. And that's not the reason I won't print your story," Shu said with a hint of invitation to follow-up from Dorothy.

"Then what is?" Dorothy asked desperate for an answer.

Shu replied with, "The story is nowhere close to being finished. I need a complete story if I'm going to print it in my magazine."

"Well then, why don't you finish it?" asked Dorothy.

"Because you are. I'm too old to get out and get the stories anymore," Shu explained.

Shu hobbled over to a peanut can he had stuffed behind a stack of old magazines. He opened it and pulled out a roll of cash. "Here take this. This should help you get started on finding the truth behind your story," Shu said as he offered up the money to Dorothy.

"Uncle. I can't. What if the story turns out to not be about a real dragon like you hope? What if it is only about a drug ring of the Tong Gang? I can't take your money knowing I might return with something you didn't expect," Dorothy pleaded.

"The truth has a funny way of never meeting our expectations. I only ask that if you take this money, you will not stop until you find the truth. No matter where the story takes you. Even if it is to a fire-breathing dragon," Uncle Shu said with a wink at the end.

Dorothy went to grab the cash and put it in her pocket. "Thank you, Uncle. I'll bring you back a page turning story.", Dorothy promised.

"Oh, I have no doubt about that.".

CHINESE MEDICINE

Issue 4

The next morning, Dorothy made her way through Chinatown with her camera around her neck and pad and pencil in her pocket. First stop, Mr. Lee's Meat Shop. Why? Mr. Lee knew or at least knew of everyone in Chinatown. He was the perfect person to start off the investigation into the letter on the Blue Dragon.

Dorothy entered Mr. Lee's shop. Her presence was made known by the ringing of a small brass bell that hung just above the door but was low enough to be hit every time someone entered. Mr. Lee didn't bother raising his head to see who had entered. He planted his feet in one spot between the chopping board behind the hanging ducks and the cash register. He pivoted between the two as he did for Mrs. Ming, who was waiting on him to wrap her chicken livers in parchment paper.

Dorothy waited in line behind Mrs. Ming with her pad in one hand and pencil in the other. She was at the ready to write down any leads that Mr. Lee might have for her. As he wiped the red juices dripping from his fingertips onto his front apron, he asked, "Are you here to buy anything or are you just making a shopping list for tomorrow?"

Dorothy realized that Mr. Lee was speaking to her even though he had not yet finished checking Mrs. Ming out.

"Oh, I was actually here to ask you if you had any leads on a story I'm chasing down," replied Dorothy.

"Story, huh. So, the *Chronicle* finally decided to give you a shot at being a journalist, did they?" Lee retorted.

"Actually I'm working for my Uncle Shu now," Dorothy said with an abruptness as to imply her desire to not go into the background behind her job change. After a short pause, Dorothy concluded that Mr. Lee had received her intent and continued to ask him what she had come there for. "I came here to see if you had heard anything about a shipment of Blue Dragon coming into San Francisco."

"Blue Dragon? I wouldn't know, but Mrs. Ming here could tell you all about it," he said.

Mrs. Ming looked back at Mr. Lee with a gaze of annoyance as if she just wanted to get chicken livers and get out. Nonetheless, Mrs. Ming was all about appearances. Her husband ran one of the busiest restaurants in Chinatown. Not wealthy enough to be considered upper class, but Mrs. Ming believed she could keep up the image to convince others that they were. In an attempt to keep with her hard-earned image, Mrs. Ming turned around with a forced smile of elegance and a high-pitched reply, "He is right. I spend quite a fortune on the stuff. Though it is worth the purchase. Mr. Ming says I've turned back the hands of time ten years."

"Excuse me for my ignorance, but what are you saying exactly?" Dorothy asked with a bit of confusion.

"My skin of course. Isn't it obvious? My face has the firmness of a porcelain tea pot ever since I started using the stuff," Mrs. Ming boasted.

Dorothy was still a little confused, as she examined the deep wrinkles on Mrs. Ming's face moving in an out as she yammered on about her appearance. "So you're saying Blue Dragon is a facial crème?" Dorothy asked.

"Crème, no. Medicine powder, yes. I buy from the limited supply at Wan Mao's. It works magic," Mrs. Ming exclaimed.

Dorothy began to smile, as Mrs. Ming had just given her the next lead. "Thank you so much for your help!" Dorothy shouted as she turned away from the conversation before Mrs. Ming could yammer on any further.

Dorothy headed out of Mr. Lee's shop, ringing the brass bell once more. She pranced down the sidewalk with a spring in her step, heading to the corner where Wan Mao's Chinese medicine store sat. The store was a grid of wood painted red with glass inlays tucked tightly into the corner of the Chinatown block. Dorothy stepped into the store, and scanned the wall, which was stacked with apothecary styled jars filled with all types of traditional Chinese medicines like Tiger's tooth.

"Welcome, how may I help you?" a young man asked from behind the counter.

"Yes, I was looking to see, if you carried the new Blue Dragon powder everyone is talking about," said Dorothy.

The young man had a nervous look of worry on his face as he looked around the store. "Blue Dragon? I don't know what you're talking about. If you're looking for lift, I have a new supply of jade rollers in the back that just came in," the man stated with a crackle in his voice. He went over to the curtain to the back room after lifting the counter pass through to allow Dorothy to come back through to look with him.

Dorothy found this unusual until she realized that the man had assumed, she was looking to buy a product for a facial lift. *How could he have known that without first knowing about the fabled benefits of this Blue Dragon that she was asking about?*

Dorothy followed the man to the back out of curiosity in, what he was going to show her. As soon as the two were at the other end of the back room, he quickly turned around and inquired about Dorothy's knowledge of Blue Dragon.

"Who told you, that we sold Blue Dragon?"

"It was Mrs. Ming," said Dorothy.

"I knew she wasn't going to be able to keep her mouth shut," he muttered under his breath.

"What are you saying? You do sell Blue Dragon?" Dorothy prodded.

"We have a limited supply," the man explained.

"Where do you get it from?", Dorothy asked. The man started to withdraw from the conversation. He still wore the nervousness on his face that he showed behind the counter.

"Why are you interested in Blue Dragon? You are still young and pretty. You should have no need for it," the man replied in an attempt to halt the inquiry.

Dorothy noticed that the man was attracted to her and used this to her advantage to keep digging for more information. Dorothy went to grab the man's forearm gently. "Why are you so nervous? I just want to buy some Blue Dragon for my mother, and heard you sell it. Can't you help a girl out?" Dorothy asked as she moved closer in with a flirtatious step.

"Look, I wish I could help you. I really do, but we aren't supposed to be selling Blue Dragon. My Dad doesn't even know that I'm selling it out of his shop," the man explained.

"So are you afraid your dad will find out? Is that it?" she asked.

The man replied, "Not my dad. I can't have the Tong Gang finding out that I've been selling their Blue Dragon out of my dad's shop."

Tong Gang, Dorothy thought to herself. *The letter mentioned the Tong Gang. I must be getting closer.*

"What does the Tong Gang have to do with make-up?" she asked.

"Nothing. The Blue Dragon powder isn't a medicine. It's a drug. The Tong Gang brings in new shipments at the port weekly. My cousin Wan Yao works the docks and pulls a bottle for me off the top. The Tongs can't find out, or me and my cousin are dead," he explained.

"Then why does Mrs. Ming use it as facial powder?" Dorothy asked.

"She's gullible, she'll believe anything I tell her," he answered.

"These shipments, when do they come in?", Dorothy questioned.

"Thursday nights, around midnight. I wouldn't get involved with the Tong Gang. They're a rough bunch," he warned.

"I can handle myself," she informed as her stature moved from flirtatious to rigidly upright.

Dorothy had gotten the information she needed and began to head out of the back room. Just a she turned; the man grabbed her wrist causing her to turn back around. "If you get caught, you didn't hear any of this from me," he demanded in a weak and scared voice.

"Don't worry. Mum's the word. But if I were you, I would stop stealing from the Tongs. It's just a matter of time before they catch your cousin," she said in a firm but calm tone before ripping her wrist away from the man.

THE DOCKS

Issue 5

It was Thursday night. Dorothy had her old brown leather women's flight jacket placed in her lap at dinner with her parents. She had been given it as a gift by her grandfather when she told him that Amelia was her hero after she became the first female to cross the Atlantic in 1928. Upon finishing their meal, her father asked her why she had her jacket with her.

"What's the deal with the jacket? Do you plan on going out tonight?" her dad asked.

"As a matter of fact, yes. Ying invited me over for after dinner tea at her apartment. I was going to stay with her tonight to catch up," Dorothy stated as she had planned to do, if her parents had asked.

"What fun! That sounds like a swell plan," her dad opined.

After dinner, Dorothy stood up from their makeshift dinner table to put on her jacket. "I'll see you all tomorrow night," Dorothy reminded as she stepped out the door of their apartment onto the landing of the fire escape outside in the back alleyway.

Dorothy didn't take her camera with her this time, as it would have alerted her parents to her lie about staying at Ying's. When she reached the bottom of the steps to the guttered ground below, Dorothy lifted an old pallet up off the brick wall that covered her dad's bike. Dorothy's choice of trousers and oxford shoes favored her well in this situation, as she cycled off with ease down the streets that were dimly lit from the lantern lights hanging above.

The ride to the docks from Chinatown was a strenuous one. Dorothy arrived just as the eight o'clock ship was being unloaded. Dorothy hopped off her bike and walked it alongside the dark edges of the fishery warehouse near the fenced edge of the port entrance. The crew didn't notice her, and she found a stack of large wooden spools and crates to hide behind until midnight. She sat down on top of a short stack of wooden pallets with her head leaning back against the metal hangar door to the fishery. There was a sliver, an opening, in the crates just wide enough to allow her to keep her eye out for the arrival of the Blue Dragon cargo ship.

It was cold outside. Dorothy's jacket was only enough to keep her torso warm. Her legs had goosebumps from the chill of the night air crawling up the wide leg of her trousers. Water, which formed from the night fog that invaded the docks as it charged from the bay, was dripping off the curved edges of the overhung roof of the fishery. The water splattered the crates next to her, sometimes hitting the side of her arm. Dorothy pulled her legs up to her chest as she did when bathing in her tub, this time to keep herself warm until midnight.

As she faced the misery of her current situation, she began to question the motives of her driving force. Why would she sit in the cold, night air surround by the smell of fish for hours, all to chase down a story from one of hundreds of letters that had come through the mail room of the *Chronicle*? What about this story was so important? Was it the story? No. I mean, the story was intriguing definitely. But she would have chased another story just as easily. What was it then? Did she feel like she had to prove herself? Yes. Well maybe, only at first. Maybe not. Dorothy had had a passion for telling stories and finding out the truth before anyone ever doubted her. Proving one's self can only come, if you have someone you have to prove yourself too. Why would she need to prove

herself, if no one doubted her in the first place? Then it hit
her. She wasn't there because this story was different. She
wasn't there because she had to prove that a woman was
capable of a man's job. She was there because that's who she
was. She loved finding stories and sharing them with people.

The peace of figuring out the root of her passion put
an ease to her that took away the disturbance of the night air.
Dorothy leaned her head against the back of the metal door
and looked up at the night sky. There was one star shining
through the cloud cover. Dorothy's eyes began to feel heavy as
they slowly closed. She drifted off to sleep.

BANG! Dorothy awoke suddenly, but without
making a sound. She hunkered her head down and peered
through the opening in the crates to see what was going on.

"Take him to the boss!", Dorothy heard faintly as she
was moving her head from left to right to widen her view
through the opening. Then she saw two suited Tong gangsters
holding a young man up by the arms. He had blood running
down one of his legs. He could barely stand. The gangsters
were holding him up; otherwise he would have fallen straight
to the ground.

They brought him to the loading ramp of a new ship
in the port, where some grungy-looking men were unloading
some wooden crates. Dorothy looked down at a pocket watch,

that she had pulled from her jacket pocket. She couldn't see very well in the dim light but could make out a thick, shadowy line pointing to the top of the watch. It was midnight! This must be the shipment, that the man from the medicine shop had spoken about!

Dorothy put the watch back into her jacket pocket and pressed her face against the edges of the crates, hoping that she would be able to get a better look.

"What do we have here?" she could hear coming from a man with a weaselly voice.

"We found him trying to snatch a crate," one of the brutes holding him up replied.

"So you think you can steal from the Hip Song Tong Gang now that great Mock Duck has retired?" the weaselly man asked cruelly.

Just then, one of the men unloading the crates from the ship tripped and dropped one on the ramp. "Careful with those! That merchandise has already been purchased." yelled the weasel. "Make sure the absinthe and one crate of the Blue Dragon gets to Mr. Henry's estate before the party tomorrow night," he continued to command.

Mr. Henry's party? Could he be talking about Arthur Henry of the San Francisco Chronicle? Dorothy thought to herself.

"Sir, what should we do with him?" asked one of the goons holding up the man with a shot leg.

"Lose him in the Bay," the weasel man directed.

Before Dorothy could blink, she watched the goon pull a gun from his jacket and shoot the man in the head. The horror of what she witnessed made her jolt back from the crates. As she did, her body naturally wanted to make her scream in fright, but she lifted her hand to her mouth to bite her thumb. In the reaction her shoulder hit a wobbly pallet leaning against the hangar door, which caused a commotion loud enough for the Tongs to hear.

"What was that?" the goon asked.

Dorothy's heart was pounding. She had thought she would be next. "Don't mind that, you fool. It's probably just some rats you scared when you fired your gun. Now get rid of that body before the police show up. I'll meet you all back at headquarters," demanded the weasel.

Dorothy waited for the trucks to leave the port before she left the cover of the crates. A soon as she heard the trucks bounce over the gate rail entrance to the docks, Dorothy came out from behind her hiding spot and ran to grab her bike. She had never peddled so fast in her life. It wasn't until she was out of the dock area that she began to cry as the adrenaline finally caught up with the shock. *Where to go now? Where was safe?* She knew that she couldn't return to her parent's or Ying's. Then, she remembered that Uncle Shu had kept a mattress under his desk at the magazine for late nights.

Dorothy made it to *Wang Shu's Monster Magazine*, and used a spare key hidden behind a loose brick to get into the back door. Her hand shook as she walked up the steep and narrow staircase. Dorothy went straight to the mattress with her shoes still on. She curled up with her eyes wide open, and heart still pounding, knowing that tonight could have ended much differently for her.

CONFIDENCE STITCHED IN COLOR

Issue 6

THUD! Wang Shu slammed a stack of magazines on his table in his office. The noise woke Dorothy from her slumber like the curse that wakes a mummy from its sarcophagus. *DOINK!* Dorothy's head hit the underside of the table.

"Well good morning! What are you doing here so early? Do you have my story already?" asked crazy Shu.

"No. I'm just getting started, But I'm hot on the trail. Maybe too hot," murmured Dorothy at the end.

"What's that? You found the dragon?" asked Shu.

Dorothy went to rub the top of her head, where a knot was beginning to form, as she replied, "Of course not. I mean, yes. I found the Blue Dragon, but it's no fire-breathing monster. It's a drug. And the Tongs are shipping it in from the ports."

Hee-who-who-hee, giggled Shu. "What are you laughing about?" Dorothy asked perplexed.

"If all you can see of a rat is its tail sticking up in the mud, do you call it a worm or a rat?" riddled Shu.

"Uncle, I think you've confused Confucius on that one," Dorothy retorted.

"Do not name your beast before you see more than just its tail. To know what your story is about, you must first find its head," Shu sung.

"Well then, I'll have to get into Mr. Henry's party tonight if I want to chase my rat's tail all the back to this story's origin," Dorothy told her uncle.

"Party! Party! Oh how I love parties!" Shu began to shout. Shu cranked up his phonograph and dropped its needle. Then he slid over to Dorothy and swung her around the room, knocking over stacks of magazines in the process. Dorothy began to cackle at her uncle's crazy personality and wobbly dance moves.

"You're quite mad, aren't you?" Dorothy asked with a smile so wide on her face that her flat cheeks began to scrunch up into cushions on the side of her face. Uncle Shu stopped spinning Dorothy and stared right back at her with a quiet blank look on his face.

"Oh Uncle, I didn't mean...", Dorothy began to apologize.

"Mad! Mad! *Who-hee-hee-hee.* The only one mad here is you if you think you're getting into a party dressed like this.", Shu said as he pulled the sides of Dorothy's trousers out like the sides of a wide road map.

"Ah! Shu!" Dorothy shrieked, hitting her Uncle in the arm for making fun of her clothes.

"Don't you worry one-bit, little Dorothy. I've got just the trick to fix this right up!" Shu claimed as he began to scavenge behind his phonograph accidently knocking the needle off the track. "Here it is!" Shu gleaned as he turned around with a fresh new issue of the *Monster Magazine.*

"Anubis – Death on the Nile," Dorothy read, "What am I supposed to do with this?"

"Go down to Hank's, give this magazine to him, and tell him that Wang Shu sent you for a dress in exchange for a free year of subscriptions," Shu directed.

"Okay, but I don't think some guy will give away a nice dress in exchange for twelve of your Monster Magazines," Dorothy stated.

Dorothy didn't question Shu any further, as she was hoping her uncle was right. She loved the way she dressed. It was comfortable, practical, and was in line with her strong and persistent personality. That didn't mean that she didn't often dream about dressing elegantly to have others look at her like her father saw her: a beautiful person.

Dorothy started to daydream on her walk to Hank's dress store. She tried to picture herself in all the different kinds of colors they could have. Red, blue, green, yellow, or maybe even a pattern would suit her best. Just as she had finished trying on all the colors in her mind, she approached Hank's.

There was a semi-circular bay window next to the store entrance in which she could see a long, green silk dress with pleats streaming down it from the neckline. In the crevasses a shimmering silver thread was woven in the silk, showing itself in the pattern of a poem tapped out in Morse code. Dorothy's hand froze on the doorknob to the shop, as she was caught in a trance looking at the beauty of the dress mystifying her through the window.

Dorothy's gaze was interrupted by Hank's smile from behind the dress in the store. He had caught Dorothy admiring the dress in the store window and called her into the store with an unreadable look on his eyes. Almost like a friendly spider inviting a fly into its web for a tea party. Dorothy opened the door and stepped in with a reservation about herself. She still didn't know if Uncle Shu's plan would work or not.

"How may I help you!" Hank asked in a bubbly manner.

"My Uncle Shu sent me with an offer," Dorothy said quietly.

Dorothy felt out of place. She had more courage facing down the Tong Gang than she did standing in the middle of Hank's dress shop.

"An offer, you say! How exciting!", Hank exclaimed. "Tell me, what is this offer?" he asked.

Dorothy pulled out the rolled-up monster magazine from her deep pockets. "A free year's subscription to Monster Magazine in exchange for a dress for me," Dorothy offered as she awaited his response.

Hank put the back of his wrist on his hip, as if he had a single chicken wing sticking out to the side. There was a pause before he reached to grab the magazine out of Dorothy's hand with the speed of a pecking ostrich in the outback. "Anubis – Death on the Nile. Oh, he will absolutely love this! You can tell your uncle, we have a deal," Hank stated. Hank had such a colorful personality; it was starting to rub off on Dorothy as her natural confidence began to return.

"So let's get down to business. What event are we trying to make you sparkle for?" Hank asked as he grabbed Dorothy's hand to pull her into the middle of the store, where there was more room to look her over. Hank began to walk around Dorothy with one arm folded into his gut, while the other rested on his folded arm to support his chin as he looked Dorothy's body up and down.

"Well, there's a party.", Dorothy said.

"Party! Now, we're talking darling. I will make you the life of the party," Hank proclaimed. Hank rushed over to a wall of shelves stacked with boxes. He pulled one out and opened it in front of Dorothy. "How about we try this little piece on?" Hank toyed.

"Oh, I don't know.", Dorothy said.

"None sense, you'll look red-hot in this," Hank argued with reassurance.

Dorothy grabbed the dress out of the box and headed to a closet room in the back where she could change into it. Hank went over to the front door of his store to lock it. He flipped a sign saying "Sorry, we're closed" over. "We mustn't have anyone disturb us. There's a masterpiece in the making!" Hank explained. After taking some time to put on the dress, Dorothy emerged with the red dress on. Hank was waiting for her with a measuring tape laid around his neck like an unwoven scarf. "Oh sweetie. This is it. You are going to knock them dead," Hank flattered.

Dorothy went over to the mirror to look at herself. After a few seconds of allowing her to check out the dress on herself, Hank approached Dorothy from behind to admire how wonderful the dress looked on her.

"There won't be an eye that doesn't notice you," Hank stated. Dorothy looked at Hank through the mirror to talk to him standing behind her.

"Well you see, the thing is I can't be noticed. There's someone at the party, I don't want to know that I am there.", Dorothy explained.

"Well honey, that's going to be quite hard. I'd have to put you in a burlap sack to dull down your natural beauty. You are just too stunning!" Hank trifled.

"You're too kind, but it really is imperative, that all I do is blend in," Dorothy noted.

"Well your request is a drag. My bones ache to make you shine, but I accept the challenge!" Hank remarked.

The next two hours were filled with a montage of empty boxes, ranges of colors, and twirls in the mirror as Dorothy tried on a collection of dresses that Hank had picked out for her. With each dress, you could see a piece of reservation fall off Dorothy's expression, to be replaced with a self-awareness and confidence in her own beauty. Hank's commentary flowed over Dorothy like a waterfall of positivity. The strong and beautiful Dorothy that had always been there had returned to show her face in public once again.

Dorothy stood in front of the mirror this time with her hair down and both hands on her hips as she turned her torso to see how magnificent she looked. Hank realized at this point, that she had regained her confidence, and stepped in to push her limits on more time.

"Are you sure you want to stay hidden at this party.", Hank asked?

Dorothy took a moment to respond as she thought about Hank's question, while admiring herself. "You know what, forget what I said before. Bring me a dress made for me. I want to gleam," Dorothy responded.

Hank smiled from ear to ear upon hearing Dorothy's response, as if he was waiting to hear her say just that. "Just a moment, then," Hank said.

Hank went over to the pleated green and silver dress hanging on the mannequin in the window. "What do you say we give this one a try next?" Hank asked.

Dorothy's eyes lit up with excitement. "Are you sure? That dress looks a little more expensive than a year's worth of Monster Magazines," Dorothy asked.

"Actually, I would say it is an even trade. Your uncle's magazines bring the same smile to my nephew's face that this dress is bringing to yours. It isn't about the money," Hank declared.

"Oh, thank you so much!", Dorothy shouted as she leapt off the wooden stand in front of the mirror to go give Hank a hug.

"Darling, you're going to make my heart melt," Hank claimed as he smiled back at Dorothy.

"Hank, do you mind if I ask you a personal question?" Dorothy prodded.

"Of course, love," Hank returned.

"You don't like women, do you?" she asked.

"What, of course I love women. I love everyone," he added quickly.

"That's not what I mean.", she explained.

"I see. Well no, not in that way," he revealed.

"Why don't you have anyone to share all your love and positivity with then? You would change the world for that special someone," she stated.

"You are too kind. However, we live in a world that is too afraid to see the beauty in everyone. Until that changes, I'm afraid people like you and me are limited to sharing our beauty with those who are willing to see it," Hank spoke, this time with a softer tone.

"Well, chin up Hank. I'm going to change the world; you just wait and see. I'll make it so that you can share your beauty with more than just those who pass through these four walls of your dress shop," Dorothy promised.

"I have no doubt of that.", Hank said, as he slid his right-hand down Dorothy's arm to her left hand to give it an endearing squeeze.

BLIND TIGER PARTY

Issue 7

It was Friday night. Mr. Henry's party was just around the corner. Dorothy was up in her room getting ready for the night. There was a broken hand mirror hanging on a rusty nail in the wall. She sat on the end of her bed in front of the hand mirror brushing her hair as she sat reflective in front of her own reflection. Hank's dress was hanging on her jacket hanger on another nail next to the hand mirror. Dorothy reached over to rub the silk of the dress between her thumb and other fingers.

"Dorothy, dinner's ready!" she heard her mother call from downstairs. Dorothy put on her dress and came downstairs.

"My goodness! Little Dorothy. Don't you look gorgeous," her father remarked.

"Thanks. Uncle is taking me to a party with some old friends at the *Chronicle*," Dorothy explained.

"Party? You're not going to a speak-easy, are you?" her mother asked.

"What? No, of course not. It's a dinner party, so I probably won't eat dinner. More for you two," Dorothy added.

"Sounds like it will be a smashing good time," her father said right before Dorothy headed out to meet her uncle.

Uncle Shu was waiting in his old Ford Model T with the black paint peeling off the side from over twenty years of wear and tear. The engine was rumbling, and the headlights were fluttering in and out from Shu sitting idle for a few minutes, as he waited on Dorothy.

"Hey Uncle," Dorothy said as she reached to open the door handle to the car. The noise startled Uncle, as his eyesight was too poor to see Dorothy approaching in the night.

"Ah Dorothy, I see Hank decided to take my offer. You look wonderful!" Shu exclaimed.

"Thanks," Dorothy remarked as she closed the passenger side door.

Uncle honked the horn twice before heading out towards the party. It was completely unnecessary though, as most of the street was empty at this time of night. As they neared Mr. Henry's house, the streets began to climb higher with the hills. The model T struggled, gasping for gas as its wheels slowly turned up the hilly grade. They finally made it to his estate. A newly installed bronze art deco gate lined either side of a pebbled drive back to his home. Shu drove through all the way up to a fountain centered in a turnaround drive in front of the front door's exterior staircase.

"How does an editor afford a place like this?" Shu muttered under his breath as he admired the stone façade that showcased the modern lines of the new architecture sweeping the nation's wealthy and elite.

"That's what I'm here to find out," Dorothy said as she stepped out of the car to go into the party. There was a line of cars waiting behind them. Dorothy turned around to make sure Uncle Shu knew when to come back to get her.

"Remember to meet me back at the gates at midnight," Dorothy reminded Shu.

Shu nodded before moseying off as the horns of the cars behind him sounded off in an inpatient push to keep the line going. Dorothy made her way up the staircase before she was stopped at the door by what appeared to be the maître d' of the party.

The man stated, "I don't believe you are on the list of guests this evening."

Dorothy paused with her posture rigid, before relaxing back after an epiphany for her response. "Well, of course I'm not on the guests list, I'm with the entertainment for tonight," she claimed.

The man looked her up and down to verify the legitimacy of her claim. "Then you must know that entertainers use the side entrance," said the maître d' as he pointed to the left side of the home with a flat palm covered in a white glove.

"Of course.", Dorothy replied as she began to walk along the front stone patio that wrapped around the massive mansion.

Dorothy made it to the end of the front of the house. It was darker, since the gas lanterns and interior light radiating near the front entry was much farther away now. As Dorothy turned the corner, she saw a dark alleyway created from the fifty tall Italian Cypress trees planted alongside the three-story home, which stretched back for what looked like three hundred feet. In the middle of the dark stretch was a glow of light pouring out of a service side door. Dorothy saw three women making their way into the side entrance. Dorothy hurried down to the door so that she could follow the ladies into the home.

Right as the side door was about to swing closed, Dorothy slid through just behind the ladies who had entered before her. They paid no attention to Dorothy, who was now just behind them. The women walked down a hall that looked more like the servant's quarters of the massive estate. There was a wooden door to the left with scuff marks at its base. The three women walked straight to the door as if this wasn't their first time entertaining for Mr. Henry's parties. Dorothy decided not to follow the three into the door but turned her head as they passed by. Inside were other women, who looked like they had arrived earlier than the others. They were all getting ready for their show. They were cabaret girls from the looks of their scanty show outfits.

Dorothy continued down the hall to a more ornate door at the end, where the noise of pompous laughter and music was seeping through the cracks. She opened the door to a great living room, that looked more suitable as the foyer to the Balboa theater. The extravagance of the brass and stone murals encapsulated along the top edges of the wall distracted Dorothy for a brief moment, before she remembered the purpose of her attendance to this event. *Blue Dragon.* That is why she was there. She needed to find the Blue Dragon crate that the Tong Gang had delivered for this party.

Right as she was about to make her rounds around the room to see if any of the guests were indulging themselves with the fabled drug, the music stopped, followed by the dimming of the lights. The crowd looked to the stage setup for the band in front of the large windows that scaled the full height of the three-story room. Then there it was, the grimy-voice Mr. Arthur Henry echoing through the chrome plated microphone. "Welcome, my beloved troupe, are you ready to indulge in the proclivities of your sinful flesh?" he announced from his platform. The crowd cheered in a roar to show their excitement for the night. "Well then, without further ado, let the debauchery commence!"

Right then, the band kicked the music back off with a trumpet blast as twelve waiters dressed in duck tails came out from the edges of the room. Six of them were carrying platters of empty crystal cocktail glasses with a small vial filled with blue powder. The other six followed behind with large crystal decanters filled with green absinthe. The waiters with the trays set the platters down on six round tables spread throughout the room. The waiters behind them, then filled the glasses with the absinthe. It wasn't long before the crowds of the rich descended upon the offering like pigs around a trough of slop.

Dorothy headed towards one of the tables in an attempt to snag one of the vials of Blue Dragon off the trays. As Dorothy approached, all the glasses of absinthe were already claimed, leaving a half-empty jar of Blue Dragon alone on a wide silver serving tray. Dorothy picked up the tray and began to head towards the door on the other side of the room, where she presumed the butler's pantry was as it was the door the waiters disappeared into. Right as she was pushing past the crowd, Dorothy was halted by a firm grip on her forearm that was carrying the tray.

"Well, well, well. What do we have here?", the voice was clearly from Arthur. Dorothy didn't even bother turning around. None the less, Arthur made his way around to the front of Dorothy to block her path to the pantry. "Dorothy Summers. What are you doing at my party?" Arthur asked condescendingly.

"What? You don't even know, who your own staff hires to service your parties," Dorothy replied cunningly.

"You know, when I said I would gladly be your first customer, this isn't what I had in mind," Arthur jeered. The men with him gave a laugh at his ghastly humor. Dorothy didn't give him the satisfaction of a response, which seemed to

annoy Arthur. "Like I asked before, what are you doing?"
Arthur seemed more annoyed now.

"I'm getting another round of glasses for your guests.",
Dorothy remarked.

"There's no need to run away with this now is there?",
Arthur said as he picked up the half-full vial of Blue Dragon.
Dorothy briefly thought she had just lost her chance to grab a
sample of the drug, before Arthur continued to slur his
drunken commands. "Make sure you top off the Blue Dragon,
after you get another round of glasses," Arthur demanded.

"Yes sir. Exactly where would I find the extra Blue
Dragon?" Dorothy asked as if she was just a small-minded
woman servant.

"In the crate in the garages, of course. Didn't the
maître d' tell you?" Arthur asked with a growing impatience, as
Dorothy was now distracting him from his own party.

"He did. I just forgot. I will get it right away," Dorothy
promised as she tilted the tray to her side to pass by Mr.
Henry.

The second Dorothy made it through the door, she
tossed the tray on top of the table in the center of the butler's
pantry before taking a deep breath. She went out the side door
to the right side of the home. The gravel drive looped around

the house. Dorothy followed the drive to the back of the home, where she came upon a four-car garage with wooden carriage doors. One of the doors was open, with the doors swung out. A dim light was leaking out from inside. The crunch of the gravel underneath Dorothy's shoes beat in pattern with her heartbeat as she came one step closer to the crate of the Blue Dragon.

Then as she turned the corner, there it was. The crate broken open, split in two by the light hanging above the empty parking space. Dorothy went to the crate and knelt so that she could search through the loosely packed hay in order to find another vial. She rummaged through the crate, all the way down to the bottom. Nothing. It was empty. Just as Dorothy thought she had reached a dead end, misfortune struck again. Dorothy leaned back to sit on the heels of her shoes, when she saw a stamp on the side of the crate. It read, "*S.S. President Hoover* – Shanghai".

Dorothy began to think about this clue. *What was this?* S.S. President Hoover*? That wasn't the ship, she saw the Tong Gang unloading. It made sense though. The* Hoover *traveled from Shanghai to Kobe to San Francisco. It was the most direct route to funnel illegal small cargo to the Americas. The letter she found was from Shanghai, too. There must be a connection. I can't figure out the missing pieces unless I can get on the* Hoover.

Just as Dorothy was unraveling the mystery to the next chapter, she heard a huge crash and glass breaking in the house. It startled her out of her deep, contemplative state. Then she heard whistles chirping up and down the sides of the home. She stood up to rush to the corner of the house to peer around to see what all the commotion was about. There she saw a team of coppers rushing in the side entrance. Dorothy knew she wouldn't make it back through the house, so she darted towards the tall cypress trees. Her silk dress snagged on the side of a branch. It did not slow her as she continued to press forward, while her dress ripped down the side fraying the silk. She began to run through the lawn of Mr. Henry's neighbor. It felt like a full minute of running before Dorothy made it to the road, where she saw Uncle Shu waiting in his Ford Model T just a few addresses down.

Dorothy ran over to Uncle Shu who was passed out in the driver seat. She woke him up when she hopped into the passenger seat and commanded him to drive. Shu's snoring was abruptly interrupted by a gasp from the noise of the car door slamming shut.

"Ah, Dorothy. Your dress is ripped," Shu pointed out.

"Yeah I know. Now let's go, quick," Dorothy demanded.

"Alright, just give me a second," Shu requested as he hopped out of the vehicle to give it a crank. "So, did you find, what you were looking for?" Shu asked as his old arms attempted to crank-start the old car.

"No, but I have my next lead.", she replied.

"Where to this time?", Shu asked.

"Shanghai, on board the *Hoover*," Dorothy said with a determination to hunt this story down to the end. Shu gave a smile before the car fired up.

S.S. PRESIDENT HOOVER

Issue 8

Dorothy had a canvas duffle bag packed with two weeks' worth of food, a bar of soap, and a single change of clothes. She was back in her normal wear, with her camera around her neck and was standing back down by the ports. Uncle was driving off back to Chinatown. The docks were crowded, and the brisk morning air was filled with the chatter of the crowd and the seagulls soaring above waiting for the fishing boats to arrive with their daily breakfast trimmings.

The *S.S. President Hoover* was stationed in the port. Dorothy pulled the ticket for her passage out of her pocket to check if she still had it. She had purchased it from the Dollar Line salesman stationed in Chinatown just the day before.

Dorothy made her way through the crowd to the boarding gangway. It was there that she handed her ticket over to the purser of the ship. As she walked up the gangway, she felt a sense of butterflies form in her stomach. It wasn't nervousness though. It felt like freedom. For the first time in her life she was stepping away from her little world in San Francisco to embark on a journey. It wasn't just any journey though. It was a journey set upon by following her own passion, a passion to find and tell stories that would never be known without people like her.

After she made it to the top of the gangway, Dorothy decided to walk along the side of the ship. She found an open spot to nestle into. She watched as the *Hoover* pulled out of port and around the bay. In front of the mountainside covered by the lush green trees, was the beginnings of the construction of the Golden Gate Bridge's North Tower. Dorothy marveled at the sight of what was possible for humans. She thought back to Uncle's imagination for the impossible. She didn't think that what she was chasing down would be another story about monster folklore, but maybe it could be something more than another international drug ring.

As the ship made its way out into the open ocean, Dorothy decided to go inside to settle her belongings in her cabin. Her room was in one of the smaller cabins, near the crew's quarters. Even though Uncle was financing the trip, his magazines didn't bring in thousands. She would have to be frugal in her search for the truth.

Dorothy spent most of the day on the first day of cruising in her dimly-lit room, scribing in her journal all that she had found so far in the story of the Blue Dragon. She detailed everything from the cloth letter, to the shooting at the docks, all the way to the blind tiger party. As she wrote it all down in a cohesive manner, the story became clearer to her. It was as if writing out the trail of clues revealed the link between it all for her. It was the reassurance she needed to know, that she was headed in the right direction, and wasn't just taking a two-week cruise to Shanghai for nothing.

There was a clock on the bedside table in the room. It read nine past seven. Dinner was at eight. Dorothy made herself ready to head down to dinner. She made her way downstairs to C deck, where the dining room was. She approached the maître d to be seated at her table.

She was seated at a four-top with three other guests. They were a young couple on a honeymoon and a fastidious British businessman. Dorothy went to go sit down in her seat. The businessman had already been at his seat for quite some time. She could tell by the dried milk at the center of the stirring spoon placed on the saucer next to his tea.

She greeted them as she sat down. "Evening," she said. The businessman looked up from his Jules Verne novel-*20,000 Leagues Under the Sea*-just enough to view Dorothy with his left eye. His other stayed hidden behind his nose, most likely never leaving the page of his book. The couple in the other two seats looked madly in love and were as giddy as school children. The young wife responded to Dorothy's greeting. "Evening to you, Miss," she said.

Dorothy nodded in a thanks for her acknowledging her greeting as she sat down. The young man, who accompanied the woman reached his arm across the table to introduce himself. "My name's Mickey Moone, and this is my wife Alice," he projected with a smile on his face. Dorothy shook his hand quickly, as it looked like he was about to lose his balance from leaning over the table. The businessman seemed annoyed with the bubbly attitude of his dinner guests. He was dressed in a pressed tux, while the others looked like they were in their only pair of untattered clothes.

Ignoring the British man's scoffing demeanor, Dorothy decided to get to know her other table guests. "So, what brings you two to journey on the *Hoover*?" she asked.

The other woman beamed with joy at the opportunity to taunt the news of their new marriage.

"We're newlyweds!" the wife almost screamed with joy.

"We're on our honeymoon. Off to Tokyo," the husband added.

"Tokyo?", Dorothy questioned.

"Yeah, Tokyo. We're taking a train after we spend a few days in Kobe," the husband replied.

"What about you? What brought you aboard this ship?" the wife asked in return.

"Well, I'm actually in the middle of a story. You see, I'm a journalist," Dorothy told.

"And I thought you were on your way back home," the businessman said, joining in on the conversation.

"Ah, so you do speak," the husband teased.

"Of course I do. I'm just not here to make friends," the Brit retorted.

"What are you here for, then?", Alice asked. The couple, although only married for a day or two, were participating like a pair of twins trading off sentences.

"I'm here simply on passage for business in Shanghai," the businessman replied in short.

"Business in Shanghai. What is it that you do there?" Dorothy asked.

"A woman journalist on her way to Shanghai. What exactly are you writing about?" the man questioned back.

"Very well then. I'll leave you to your Verne," Dorothy reverted as she was not ready to reveal her intentions in Shanghai to a table of strangers.

Right as the ice was broken between the four strangers, the waiter arrived with dinner. It was a white fish served with a tomato puree and string beans. The conversation slowed as the four enjoyed their meal before retiring back to their cabins.

Over the next week, Dorothy became good friends with Mr. and Mrs. Moone. She almost forgot that she was there on business. It had been three days since she had last thought about the case of the Blue Dragon. The businessman became cordial over time, but kept his head buried in a new adventure novel every night as to avoid the pre-dinner conversations.

The *S.S. President Hoover* had finally made it to port in Kobe, Japan. The Moones said their goodbyes to their new friend and told her to look them up in San Francisco when she returned. The ship received a new stock of supplies in port, including new passengers. Dorothy wondered whether her and the businessman would be assigned new dinner table guest or not.

Later that evening, Dorothy approach her dinner table to find that it would only be herself and the businessman for the remaining few days of their trip to Shanghai. This time, he was reading a new book, titled *The Werewolf of Paris* by Guy Endore.

"So, I'm assuming you have a fascination with monsters and legend folklore," Dorothy stated as she took her seat next to the British man.

The man picked up his evening tea to take a sip before responding. "It's the mysticism that enchants me into these fictional worlds," he replied.

"You sound like my Uncle. He owns a magazine back in San Francisco. He writes about monsters. You would like his stories," Dorothy said, trying to keep from the silence as they waited on their meal.

"Really now. What is the name of his publication?" the man asked, this time seeming legitimately interested.

"*Wang Shu's Monster Magazine*," Dorothy told him.

"I never heard of it during my visit to San Francisco," the man remarked.

"Most people in the city don't even know of it. He mainly sales to locals in and around Chinatown," she explained. "What is it that you do again?" she asked.

"I never said, but I guess there's no reason to keep it from you, now them we have become acquainted with one another. I'm an English publisher. Right now, I'm traveling the globe looking for places to set up print shops to expand our operations."

"Do you ever take submissions from first-time authors?", Dorothy asked.

"Depends on the material, but yes we have in the past," he said.

"Would you mind if I wrote your office address down? I'm working on a story for my uncle's magazine that I believe the world will want to know about," she asked.

"Is it about monsters too?" the man asked, lifting his book about werewolves.

"No, it's about an international drug ring that is tied back to the wealthy elite of the Western United States," she replied.

"In that case...", the man began to answer as he tore the back page out of his book to write down the address to his publishing office in London, "...send your story here once you've compiled it. I look forward to reading it," the man finished as he handed over the ripped page with fresh ink on it.

Dorothy took the page excitedly. She blew on the ink before folding the paper into her pocket. The waiter set the final dinner on their table. A seared tuna steak. Dorothy could barely eat; she was so eager to finish the story tomorrow, when they ported in Shanghai.

FAIRMONT PEACE HOTEL

Issue 9

As Dorothy stepped off the boat, she saw buildings galore. The hustle and bustle of the city reminded her of San Francisco. Except Shanghai was what she imagined San Francisco might be, if it were given a few decades to catch up. There seemed to be all kinds of people living in the city and going about their day. Shanghai was the melting pot of the East, and San Francisco was the melting pot of the West.

First thing's first, Dorothy had to find a place to stay. She decided to stay close to the river. The Tong Gang was sending shipments back to San Francisco through the bay, so her next clue had to be near the water.

Dorothy began walking along the side of the river looking for some form of familiar in this new foreign world she had entered. It was unlike anything she had ever seen. Then as all sorts of people where pushing past her speaking Mandarin, Japanese, and Wu Chinese; a white gentleman walked past her speaking English with the same accent as the publisher from the *Hoover*. The man was dressed in pin-striped pants and a blue suit jacket. He walked into a waterfront hotel with another man.

The familiarity of a language that Dorothy could understand, drew her into the hotel like a horse to water. Upon opening the door, she found the lobby filled with all types of Westerners, mostly British by the sound of them. She approached the front desk.

"Welcome to the Fairmont Peace Hotel," greeted the receptionist.

"Oh hello.", Dorothy replied a little surprised. She was so used to her fellow Americans treating her like a Chinese native that she was taken aback by the receptionist immediately treating her like an average American tourist.

"Do you have any rooms available for tonight?" Dorothy asked.

"We have a single room on the third story, river side," the receptionist offered.

"That's perfect, I'll take it," Dorothy answered.

"Alright, and how long will you be staying with us?" the receptionist continued down his list of booking questions for the hotel's ledger.

"One week," she replied.

"And whom might I ask is staying with us?" he asked.

"Oh, I'm so sorry. The name's Dorothy. Dorothy Summers," Dorothy blushed as she told him her name. She had forgotten to introduce herself when she first approached the desk. She had been so focused on the fact that she felt more welcomed at a hotel in Shanghai, than she did at her old job back at home.

"Well Ms. Summers, welcome to the Fairmont Peace Hotel. We hope you enjoy your stay. Our bellhop can help you to your room," the receptionist spoke as he stretched out his hand to the bellhop who was now standing behind her.

"May I help you with your bag, madam?" the bellhop said. He was a young boy, maybe fourteen. He looked like he was native to Shanghai but had learned English better than most people in Chinatown, San Francisco.

"Oh, sure," Dorothy muttered as she handed it over to the boy. She was perfectly fine carrying the bag herself but could tell that this job was all the boy had. She didn't want to deny him of the one chance he had at having a better life.

The bellhop took the bag, and they made their way to the elevator. The two went up in the small, brass-plated and wood-lined box. The dial on the inside of the elevator slowly traveled along its pivot to the number three. The cables stopped, and the bellhop opened the doors waiting for Dorothy to step off first. The boy walked down the hallway to room 306. He inserted the ornate key with a green tassel into the slot in the door, before entering and setting the bag at the base of the bed.

"Thank you," Dorothy said appreciatively as she handed him a few custom gold units in appreciation. The bellhop's eyes widened as he took the paper money and stuffed it into his pocket. The gratitude on the boy's face made Dorothy smile. The boy handed Dorothy the key to the room before leaving.

After the boy had left, Dorothy went to the window in her room to pull back the curtains. As she looked out her window, she could see all the wooden boats with their canopy roofs jammed alongside the Huangpu River. As she gazed over the tightly-packed streets below, Dorothy realized finding the Tong Gang's operation in this city would be more difficult than she had first thought. Now posed the question, "How do you find a needle in a haystack?"

I SPY

Issue 10

The next morning, Dorothy went downstairs to the dining room of the hotel to have a morning espresso. She had usually never been able to afford such morning routines; however, she did take a liking to coffee. She used to steal a few sips at the *Chronicle* whenever she was asked to make another brew for the journalists there.

They brewed it very strong in Shanghai, and it took Dorothy by surprise on the first sip. The caffeine rushed through her like a runaway rail train. Her eyes widened. Suddenly a rush came to her, and she began to think about the story of the Blue Dragon. *Where next? Where were the Tong Gang operating from?*

The questions led Dorothy to remember the inscription on the crate she had found at Mr. Henry's place "*S.S. President Hoover* – Shanghai". She had never found any crates in the hull of the ship during her entire two-week journey from San Francisco, but maybe the Tong Gang was only utilizing the shipping services one-way.

Dorothy began to realize her mistake. She was so enamored with the architecture, food, and other sights and smells all around the city upon her arrival, that she forgot to keep her eye on the ship as it was being unloaded and reloaded. It would be four weeks before she had another opportunity to witness the *Hoover* in port in Shanghai again, and she didn't have the cash to stay kept up in the Fairmont Peace Hotel that long.

She was going to have to either hunt down her next lead within a week or find a more affordable accommodation. As much as she would rather sit back and enjoy this beautiful city for a month, it wasn't in Dorothy's nature to sit still. She had to start poking around and turning over the rocks as they laid. The only danger with this approach was that some stones can reveal a viper when turned over. Dorothy was going to have to be careful, if she didn't want to end up on the wrong side of the story with the Tong Gang.

Which stone to up-turn first? The ports always seemed like the best spot for lots of illegal activity. Maybe someone down there had seen something or knows something about the shipments on the *S.S. Hoover*.

Dorothy paid her tab for the espresso and headed down to the port where she first came into Shanghai the previous day. As Dorothy approached, the squawks of the Vega gulls drowned out the chatter of the crowd around her. Dorothy began to think. *Who of all people working the docks, would know the most? The stevedores, probably. Yes, that's it. They should be easy to bribe for information too.*

Dorothy pushed her way past the crowd of passengers awaiting the boarding at the gangway. Just another two-hundred feet down the port terminal was the loading gangway, where a group of four dockers were busy reloading the ship with food and cargo for the ship's journey across the Southeast Asian peninsula.

As they were busy loading the ship, one of the younger dock hands looked up to see Dorothy, a beautiful woman, walking their way. He tapped the forearm of the lead docker as he was bending down to pick up the next crate. The man looked up to see what the younger boy was getting at. When he saw that it was a young woman, he stepped out from behind the line of cargo they were hauling up into the ship's hull and wiped his sweaty hands on his shirt as he walked towards her. The man spoke to her in Wu Chinese.

"Oh, I'm American. I only speak English and Mandarin," Dorothy explained, before he spoke too much more. The man began to speak English.

"I said, the passenger's gangway is back that way."

"Oh, I'm not a passenger of this ship. I'm here for information." Dorothy then flashed a wad of custom gold units at the man before returning it to her pocket for safe keeping.

"What information are you looking for?" The man seemed intrigued.

"Do you load the cargo for the *S.S. President Hoover?*"

"I'm going to have to get my hands on those gold units before I give you an answer."

Dorothy pulled out the wad, unrolled it, and then cut the stack in half before slapping it in the man's hands. "You get half now, and the other half, once I get the answers I'm looking for." The man thumbed through the stack of papers to count it as he began to tell Dorothy, what he knew.

"Yeah, we've loaded the *Hoover* before."

"Have you by chance run across a crate of Blue Dragon?", Dorothy pressed.

"Blue Dragon. What do you know of Blue Dragon?" he demanded. Dorothy got excited. She was obviously headed in the right direction. She had to conceal her emotions though.

"I know my very wealthy boss is interested in the stuff and sent me here to see if I could set up a purchase with the Tong Gang."

The man looked hesitant, as if he didn't know whether he could trust Dorothy or not. "Wealthy boss, you say. Well you can give me the other half of that paper in your pocket and come back tonight with more. Then you can tell your boss I'll get him what he needs." Dorothy pulled out the rest of the stack of cash she had slipped back into her pocket and handed it over to him. Before letting go, she gripped the cash as he was about to pull it away.

"What time?"

"Midnight, tonight. Right here."

"I'll be back."

The man put the cash straight in his pocket without counting it this time. Dorothy turned around to walk away. As she was a few strides away, she turned back to look at the man.

She saw him hand the cash over to the younger man who had noticed her at first. Then the young man ran off, as if to get the money to someone else. The others continued to load the boat.

Dorothy decided to go back to her hotel room to write out more of the article she was working on as she waited for the clock to strike midnight. She began to doze in and out of sleep, looking at the clock each time she caught herself falling asleep. This last time she woke up, the clock showed eleven forty-seven.

Shoot! Dorothy thought to herself. She only had thirteen minutes to get down to the docks. It would take her at least twenty, if she was walking fast. Dorothy grabbed her camera and a satchel she had purchased at a shop in town. She ran out of the hotel entrance in a desperate hurry to not lose her newfound lead.

She made it to the docks. Dorothy went down the length of the pier, where she had talked with the dockers. It was dark, and Dorothy couldn't tell if anyone was there with her or not. The air around them was quiet. Almost too quiet, as if it was on purpose. Dorothy decided to see, if anyone was there.

"Hello...Hello...Is anyone there?"

Just when Dorothy had thought she had missed the meet up, she heard a footstep behind her. She turned around to see who it was, but before she could...THUNK!

Dorothy was out cold. As she came back around, she could feel her body strapped in a sitting position in a chair. Her hands were behind her back. They were tied with very coarse rope that was rubbing her wrist raw. She started to open her eyes, but she had to close them quickly. There was a bright light shining down from above. She tried opening them again, this time slower while she squinted halfway.

She was in a large dark room, almost like a large empty building. A warehouse maybe? Then she heard footsteps walking her way. It sounded like wooden dress soles clapping the concrete floor in a slow, unemphatic pattern. She saw a brutish arm pierce the light above to set a wicker café chair in front of her. The man responsible for the clacking footsteps then emerged to sit down in the chair. The light only illuminated him from the bottom button of his coat jacket down.

"I've heard you have a very wealthy boss?"

"Yes."

"Well, I highly doubt that. What boss would send his employee to Shanghai to purchase a gift shop satchel and carry a worn-out camera?"

The man's hand draped down into the light, with Dorothy's camera in his clutches. The man opened the camera roll, exposing the film to the light.

"Please don't, that was a gift from my father!"

"Why don't you tell me, what you are really doing here? And who told you about the Blue Dragon?"

Dorothy knew that she couldn't reveal the truth of why she was there and how she knew about the Blue Dragon. She thought she would be as good as dead. *Maybe someone would find her story hidden in the nightstand of the Fairmont Peace Hotel, when she failed to checkout.* Dorothy decided to stay silent.

"Not talking, aye. No matter. You're American, which means no one will be able to find you here."

The brute who placed the chair asked the boss if he wanted him to get rid of her.

"No. No need to have a mess to clean up in the city. Take her to the monastery on the next resupply run. Work her in the caves there."

The boss stood up and began to walk back out the way he came in. Dorothy was anxiously waiting for what her fate may become. Before she could begin to even think of her family back home, a small burlap sack was shoved over her head. All she could see were small square holes for light to pour in through.

Dorothy felt two men grab either one of her arms to stand her up and drag her to the back of what sounded like a pick-up truck. They threw her up into the back, but her body hit a large object. It felt like a cotton bale. It was soft. Soon the smells of manure and the baaas of sheep penetrated the burlap sack over her head.

Dorothy stood her body up with her feet to place her back and tied up hands against the wooden slates on the side of the truck. For the next three hours, Dorothy was tossed back and forth in the back of the truck with the sheep as the driver journeyed outside of the city.

The air was getting thinner and thinner with each hour that passed. Dorothy didn't know if it was the sheep droppings or if they were climbing in elevation. Either way, the long journey kept Dorothy in the dark, not knowing what would await her at the end. Each second felt like a minute, and each minute felt like an hour. She counted her heart beats, until she heard the brakes on the truck screech to a halt.

MOUNTAIN MONASTERY

Issue 11

Dorothy heard the driver yell out to someone in front of her. Then the creaking of two large gate doors sounded in front of them before the driver put the truck back into gear to drive inside. The truck made a loop to turn itself around before coming to its final stop.

CLICK. The latch on the back of the truck was opened. Next the rough burlap sack scratched against Dorothy's face as it was taken off her head by one of the goons guarding the monastery.

Dorothy could now see and looked up at the large, ancient Buddhist monastery that looked to be carved into the mountainside. Then she looked behind her around the truck to get her bearings on where they were. The men were in the process of closing the gates. Dorothy could see a road with a sheer drop-off curving around the mountain. It was almost sunrise, and the early dawn light shone onto the other mountain across the ravine.

They must have driven for three or four hours outside of Shanghai and were in the mountains somewhere. She had no idea where she was. She hadn't heard or read about any monastery in the mountains around Shanghai.

Before she could look around any further, one of the Tong Gang's muscle grabbed Dorothy to escort her through the entrance to the monastery. Dorothy was memorized by the ornate carvings that looked nearly one thousand years old. She almost forgot that she was a prisoner in a foreign land.

Dorothy wasn't a Buddhist herself, but knew the Tong Gang wasn't operating here because of their faith. It didn't take long for her suspicions to be confirmed. The men escorted her into a shrine room, where a statue of Buddha that had been carved into the mountainside was halfway blown to pieces. Behind the statue was a tunnel. A dim, flickering light produce by gas lanterns hanging from hooks imbedded in the rock guided them down into the mountain.

This was a huge operation. *Why would the Tong Gang expend so much effort in concealing their new drug? It wasn't like they were taking the same effort in their trade of opium. So what about this drug was worth keeping it such a deep secret?*

As Dorothy began to ponder these thoughts in her head, the group approached a split in the tunnel. The right side continued downward, while the left side leveled out. The men pulled Dorothy to the left, where the tunnel opened into a large, carved-out room. There were metal bars embedded into the floor, splitting the room in two. It looked like a jail cell in a small-town police department.

The men pushed her into the cell before slamming the barred door shut behind her. The two then went over to a makeshift table. They sat on top of two empty dynamite crates. There was hay on the ground, where they had most likely unpacked the explosives. Maybe they used it to create these tunnels in the mountain. The two men sat down and began setting up a game of Mahjong.

"You know, you need at least three to play Mahjong.", Dorothy projected.

One of the men looked back at her before turning back around to continue setting up the board. As they got done setting up the board, two more men entered the room from the tunnels. They had black soot on their faces. The men sat their guns to the side and joined the other two around the Mahjong table.

Dorothy, who was hoping to join in on the game, didn't seem disappointed when the other two showed up to play. Their presence indicated to her that this place was on a schedule like clockwork. Everyone knew their place and knew when to be where at what time.

The only thing that did not make sense to Dorothy was the makeshift jail cell. It was obviously newly built, and by the Tong Gang itself. Yet, she was the only prisoner. *What use did they have for it before she had arrived?*

Dorothy spent the day in her cell, listening to the noises above and below her in the tunnel. She also took mental note of the comings and goings of the guards, and which guard came in around what time. She didn't see any workers, only guards, gang members. On occasion one of the men would come up the tunnel with a small crate like the one she found the Blue Dragon vial in at Arthur Henry's place.

Lunchtime had come and past, and the men in the room with her were cooking a broth noodle soup with carrots for themselves. Dorothy had asked for a bowl. Her stomach was beginning to growl. The guards responded back in their native tongue, and Dorothy didn't know if they were going to feed her or not.

After the men finished eating their supper, the skinny one with a bloated gut that stood out like a bowling ball under his shirt began to cook a large pot of rice. They couldn't have been cooking it for just her. There was enough rice to feed four people. Dorothy thought that they might have been cooking themselves a second course.

As the cook finished cooking the rice, he portioned out the pot into five small bowls. The cook handed Dorothy one of the cups with two bamboo chopsticks sticking out of the lump like a pair of incense. The other four cups were set aside. The other guards didn't look hungry, and the cups remained untouched.

Before she could finish her small cup of the rice. She heard a group of voices ascending from the tunnel below. This seemed late for there to be commotion at this hour. Two other guards entered the room with four Buddhist monks dressed in tattered, soot-covered robes.

The new guards yelled at Dorothy to get back against the wall of the cell in Wu. Dorothy complied, as she was curious about the new arrivals. She had thought she was alone, the only prisoner in this monastery camp of the Tong Gang.

The main guard who looked to be in charge, or at least the highest-ranking, opened the cell to let the four monks enter. Dorothy sat back silently to observe the hierarchy between the guards. The main one with a thin moustache yelled at the others sitting at the table. The four sitting down sprang up to grab their guns and headed out of the room. They turned left upon exiting the room to head downwards. The cook handed the monks their cups of rice before leaving.

Dorothy was eager to get to know her new cellmates. The introductions would have to wait until the morning though. Dorothy's eyelids began to fall like two heavy curtains in front of a window whose straps had slipped loose of their hooks. She was asleep.

BROTHER MONK

Issue 12

The sun rose the next morning. It was the only time of the day that the sun was at the right angle to trickle into the monastery, past the shrine, and down the first few steps of the tunnel before fading out against the light of the gas lanterns.

The healthiest-looking monk leaned over to tap Dorothy on the shoulder. The cook had just served them another cup of rice for breakfast. The healthy monk outreached his hand to offer Dorothy her cup of rice. He noticed Dorothy staring at his woven orange sleeve as it retracted back on his arm as he stretched out to give her the cup.

"Have you ever seen a Buddhist monk's garments before?"

"No. Well not on a monk, and not orange."

"Yellow and burgundy then?"

"Yes."

"Those are the colors of our Tibetan brothers."

A Tibetan monk? Could a Tibetan monk be responsible for sending the letter, that started Dorothy on her journey?

"Did a Tibetan monk ever live here at this monastery?"

The monk seemed to ignore her question as he peacefully finished his bowl of rice.

"You better finish your breakfast before they call us to work."

Before the monk could finish his sentence, the guards got up from their game of Mahjong. The youngest gang member hit the bars of the cell with a stick of bamboo he would carry around. CLACK, CLACK, CLACK! *What an annoying, loud sound.* Dorothy took this obnoxious cue as her hint to finish her rice as the monk had instructed.

She stuck her hand into the cup to scoop large portions out to stuff her face. Three large clumps of rice were packed between her cheeks like the nuts in a chipmunk's mouth. She pushed herself off the ground of the stone floor as the guard opened the cell door.

Dorothy followed the other monks out. They looked like they knew where to go. The healthy monk was still sitting on the floor. He looked like he was meditating right after his meal. The guard gave another whack against the bars with his bamboo stick. CLACK! The monk opened his eyes, stood up, and left the cell right behind Dorothy.

The group was being escorted from both the front and the back by members of the Tong Gang. They walked down the tunnel stairs. Each step was set at a different height and width with an oblique shape. It was impossible to get a rhythm going down. Dorothy had to pay attention to her feet to see where to step next.

The path down slowly winded back and forth like a slow serpent weaving through a bamboo forest. Every fifty feet or so, there would be a room carved out in the side. She imagined they would most likely be the gang's quarters, a kitchen, storage, munitions, or a number of other odd spaces useful for a criminal group like the Tong Gang.

As the group traveled lower and lower, Dorothy's head began to sink with each step. She thought to herself, *how did I get here? It didn't seem too long ago, that I was sorting through mail at the Chronicle.*

The monk behind her noticed.

"Yes.", he said.

Dorothy turned around to look at the monk.

"What?"

"The answer to your question. There was a Tibetan monk who was living with us here for a while. His name was Lhami. He was able to get away right as the Tong Gang arrived. He promised to send for help."

Dorothy's head picked up after hearing this. She knew that this monk was the one responsible for sending her the story on a piece of his garment to the *Chronicle*. She was able to follow the story all the way back to this temple. This was validation.

She was right on the trail of the story. Only a journalist would have the wits and courage to follow this story all the way to this point. She was not going to stop. She was going to find the origins of this Blue Dragon, escape the Tong Gang, and publish this story.

The story Dorothy was going to tell was about to change drastically with her next step.

BLUE DRAGON

Issue 13

Seven hundred and ninety-three steps from her cell.
Dorothy was at the bottom of the tunnel. As she looked up,
what she saw next would change her life forever. There was no
going back to the world she once knew.

The tunnel opened up to a natural formation inside
the mountain. A large cavern, a cave with a small lake split in
two by fallen stalactites. Stalagmites were coming through the
water on the edges of the fallen rock bridge. The pathway was
lit by a chain of torches. The sound in the chamber was the
echoing of an internal waterfall flowing from the ceiling of the
cave at the far end.

This of course is not what changed Dorothy
Summers, or the world as we knew it. It was what Dorothy

found with her eyes at the base of the waterfall in that cave, that made crazy Uncle Shu to not seem so crazy.

At the base of the waterfall was a living blue dragon. It looked just like the paintings and myths of the old. It laid on top of a rock plateau just in front of the waterfall.

It had four legs, all chained down with large rusty chains from a streamliner's anchor chain that were driven into the rock bed with a large iron spike. Its body winded back and forth like the tunnel they took to get there. Its body was covered in mystic, earthy blue scales the size of Dorothy's torso. There were spots up and down the dragon's body where the scales were missing, and in their place were bloody white scars.

A golden white mane of hair flowed halfway down the dragon's back from its head. In between its ears were antlers like a caribou, that had been cut and shaven down only a few feet above its head. Its snout was tied shut with large marine rope. The dragon was kept subdued by a large fire, where hay was used to sedate the dragon with a pillow of smoke. When the light bounced off the waterfall, it looked like an orange and black sword was piercing the dragon from behind.

The site of this majestic animal that Dorothy had until just now thought to be a myth, brought her a range of emotions from shock to sadness. To see this creature contained and tortured as the Tong Gang had kept it, broke Dorothy's heart. Her compassion was empathized by the monks in her company, as they were guardians of all life.

"It is okay to cry, sister," the one monk said softly as he laid his hand on her back. The small kindness comforted Dorothy. She didn't feel alone in her sadness. Before she could cry, the group was pushed along to the rocky opening, where they were keeping the dragon.

"What are we doing down here, and why have they chained that dragon up?" Dorothy asked. The questioned seemed somewhat normal, but off at the same time. Dorothy had come across a dragon for the first time. A creature once thought to be no more than folk lore, and her first question was, "Why was it chained up?"

Of course, who could blame her? The shock of such a discovery while also being led as a prisoner in a foreign land in an underground bunker wasn't normal either. Maybe Dorothy was just trying to regain some sense of normality in her life.

"They harvest the scales of the ancient creature and use us to grind the scales down into a powder.", the monk replied.

The gang moved the group past the dragon. As they passed it, Dorothy looked at the scarred tissue, where they had harvested its scales. The muscle and skin were lacerated in such a rough way. It was as if, they had chopped it off of the with an axe, the same way a novice lumberjack would hack away at the stump of a stubborn tree.

When Dorothy went past the dragon's head its eyelid was shut but at eye level with Dorothy. The dragon was asleep, but the way its eyelid rested told Dorothy more than she was ready for. This creature wasn't just sad or in pain, it was on the verge of giving up, of losing hope. It reminded her of herself, back at the *Chronicle*.

Near the end of the plateau, near the hay fire the Tong Gang was using to keep the dragon in its slumber, were two large stones. The base stone was arched like a turned-up crescent moon. On the top was another stone shape like a large wheel resting in the crescent cup of the other. A large piece of timber was fashioned through the center of the stone. It protruded the wheel on both sides.

Two of the gang members split the prisoners up, putting two of them on one side and Dorothy with the other two on the other side. Dorothy was on the side near the dragon. One of the gang members then began to chain each of their hands to the timber piece that was sticking out of the stone. There were six iron cuffs permanently affixed to the timber post, three on each side. This told Dorothy that there had been other prisoners here at one point.

The monks stood there as if the routine was second nature to them. They all turned their heads to the right, away from the dragon.

"Why are you looking that way? What are they about to do to us?" Dorothy asked nervously.

"It's not what they are about to do to us. It's about what they are going to do to the creature," one monk replied.

There it was again. The monks referred to the dragon as a creature. It was as if to them the dragon was important because it was another living being. The fact that it was a dragon didn't seem as important of a detail to them.

Dorothy couldn't look away from the dragon. She was curious as to what would pull the gaze of the monks away from what the Tong Gang was about to do. Then before she could think another thought, Dorothy witnessed the horror the monks tried to avoid.

Two gang members used crowbars to pull one of the scales of the dragon back. The effort it took seemed like the two were trying to lift a car. Once the pair had pulled the one scale back far enough, another member moved in with a rusty hatchet. He began to hack at the skin holding the scale in. He seemed to be in a race to free the scale from the dragon's body before the others lost the energy to hold the other at bay.

The strikes against the dragon's body caused the dragon to stir. It let out a soft, moaning roar. The sound was that of a prey who cried out in pain after it had already been caught by its predator. It was only out of pain that the dragon roared. It was not reactive; the dragon didn't attempt to move its body to throw the other two off of itself. It accepted its fate.

The one man with the hatchet picked the bloodied scale off the floor after his deed. He walked it over to Dorothy and the monks and placed it in the wedged area of the two stones as he picked the last bit of meat off the ends. Before she could ask the question, "Now what?" The Tong boy who carried the bamboo stick around lashed it across the monk's back next to Dorothy. The monks began to push the piece of timber in a rocking motion until it began rolling the stone over the scale. It began to crack the scale and crush it beneath the weight of the wheel. Each pass became easier and easier as the scale was refined into a mystic blue powder.

"I don't understand. Why do they keep the dragon alive? Why not just kill it and take all its scales at once? Why do they torture it so?"

"If they do not harvest them while the dragon is alive, the scales will lose the life force of the creature."

Another Monk chimed in with more information.

"The life force is what gives the scales their hallucinogenic properties."

"This creature used to have a mate, before the Tong Gang killed it," the healthy Monk added. "It wasn't until the creature had already passed that the Tongs realized their mistake. That is why this creature has lost its will to fight back."

"What about all of you? Have you all lost the will to fight back as well?"

The healthy monk looked at Dorothy with a kindness. He was the only one who carried himself with a worry-free calmness. He was calming like a steady stream of water, flowing around the obstacles laid before him. Dorothy had wondered, if the healthy monk was an enlightened one.

"There used to be other monks. They fought back, when the Tong Gang killed the other dragon, but they too lost their lives. I convinced the others to maintain a spirit of peace for the sake of life."

"Whose life? The Tongs' or yours?" Dorothy questioned.

"Neither. It is for the egg that this creature carries within its womb."

"The dragon's pregnant?"

"Yes, and it is our duty to ensure she is kept alive until it is able to lay its egg. We were able to get our Tibetan brother freed to send for help. There are magical creatures scattered across the Earth that hold the spirit of the other animals within their being. They are the mother creatures, and I'm afraid they are disappearing from our world. We monks have sworn a life to protect these creatures. Our monastery has been guarding the blue dragons for nearly a thousand years, since they were first hunted by traveling Europeans crossing through our lands."

This story was bigger than Dorothy had previously imagined. This wasn't just a story about an international drug ring, a crime syndicate, a corrupt businessman, prisoners, or even a dragon. This story was epic, and the mystery of the blue dragon was just the beginning. Dorothy knew more now than ever what her purpose was. She had to tell this story. All of it. To do so, she was going to have to get out. She needed to escape.

A HOUDINI BLUEPRINT

Issue 14

It had been a few days since Dorothy witnessed the harvesting of the dragon scale. She had not spoken to the monks about her plan on escaping. She knew their goal wasn't to get free. This monastery was their home, and their purpose was to protect the dragon above all else. Though after a few days of contemplation, Dorothy came to the conclusion that she was not going to escape without the help of the monks. Dorothy knew the healthy monk was the leader of their group. If she could convince him to help, the others would follow.

That day the Tong Gang led the group to the room where they were keeping the sheep. The boy with the bamboo stick was with them. Dorothy didn't like him. He seemed to be the worst of all the Tongs. The others were cruel with no regard for life or the ability to dignify her and the monks as other humans. However, the origin of their darkness was motivated by loyalty to the Tongs, financial gain from the drug trade, or the 'its them or me mentality'.

The bamboo boy was different. He took pleasure in the pain they caused. He actually saw them as humans, and he was okay with the pain he caused anyway. Dorothy didn't understand it. The boy had the capability for empathy. He almost knew exactly what she and the monks were going through, what they were feeling. It's when she felt him feel the most connected that he would lash out in rage.

What could cause someone, another human, to react to those feelings like that? Dorothy felt the same type of empathy for people. She could connect with them. The difference was that the connection she had drove her to compassion. She felt a desire to help those out of the situation that was causing them so much pain.

This empathy led her to not only want to escape for her own life, or to tell the story, but to also free the dragon. *That's it!* That is how she would get the monks to help. A plan to free both her and the dragon.

The group was led over to stools around the middle of the room. They were given shears, and a sheep was brought to the middle of them. The monks began shearing off the wool from the sheep, while one of them began to pray over the sheep. The act was out of place for someone like Dorothy, who had lived in the city her whole life. Once they were done, they collected the wool to bundle together. The sheep was then taken down the tunnel to be fed to the dragon. This left only one Tong member in the room standing guard by the door. Dorothy took this opportunity to talk to the monks about an escape plan.

Psst. Dorothy tried to get the attention of the healthy monk without alerting the guard. At this moment Dorothy realized she didn't know the name of the monk after all this time. One of the other monks noticed and tapped the healthy monk on the shoulder.

"Bodhi. Dorothy is trying to ask you something," the monk whispered.

Bodhi looked up to address Dorothy.

"Yes?" Bodhi whispered.

"I'm getting out of here, and I need your help."

"That is a dangerous thought. You should accept where the Universe has placed you. Be like water."

"Like water, my nature is to keep moving, no matter what obstacles are in my path. It is time for me to flow down the river. Not just me either, for the dragon too."

"What are you saying?"

"I am going to free the creature from his prison. Will you help?"

"I don't want to take part in violence. Nor is it in my nature to plan. I only react."

"Well it won't be long before too much of the life force of the dragon is taken from its scales and the egg dies. I am going to escape. If your duty is to protect the life of the creature and its future, then I ask when it is time, you react according to your nature."

The monk thought for a while about what Dorothy had just offered him. Bodhi nodded in agreement. Then the guards came back into the room to set another sheep in front of them. Dorothy and Bodhi didn't speak until later that night.

As night fell, Dorothy and the monks laid back against their cell wall with their eyes closed. They were not asleep but were listening to the echo in the tunnels. They waited until the last of the Tongs had gone to sleep. Then Bodhi woke the others as they huddled around each other to hear Dorothy explain her escape plan.

It was as dark as could be. The night sky was bright that night, though. A small dribble of light seeped down into the cell room from the tunnel. It was enough for them to see a dark blue and black silhouette of each other as they Dorothy whispered her plans to them in the circle.

Dorothy told them of her plan to escape. It would require everything they had available. The dynamite, the gas from the lanterns, some Blue Dragon, access to the Tong tea pot, and the hope that the dragon's spirit had not been completely broken. Tomorrow Dorothy was going to be free.

ESCAPE

Issue 15

It was morning. This was the day Dorothy had to
escape. It was now or never. The truck was going to come later
that afternoon, after lunch. The monks said it would always
come the day after they sheared the sheep. It was all scheduled
like clockwork.

Whatever happened next would be fate. Dorothy was
hoping that good fortune would flow her way. She sat up as
she ate her rice breakfast. She had been keen on figuring out a
way to get out of there ever since she arrived. Now that she was
about to escape, all she could think about was her old life;
from the mornings spent closing her bedroom window from
the night before, to coming down the stairs, to her Dad's loving
greeting.

Dorothy knew that the journey and choices that brought her to that cell was the right one. This was who she was meant to be, an investigative journalist. Someone who pushed the boundaries, someone who was not afraid of an adventure, and someone who could speak for those who could not speak for themselves. Although she felt she was in the right place, it was hard for her to not deny that the simple life she lived before bore comforts she was now missing.

Her daydream was interrupted by the usual hit of the bamboo. *CLANK!* The sound refocused Dorothy. Every move or thought after this point was going to be calculated. She was either going to be free or die trying.

The group was led back down the tunnel and into the cavern. They were chained to the post on the grinding wheel. This time Dorothy made sure she positioned herself at the cuff position next to the stone.

ROAR! The dragon called out in pain as the Tongs harvested yet another scale from her body. The dragon's eyes opened as her inner eyelids retracted long enough to look Dorothy in the eyes. Dorothy looked back at the dragon as she thought to herself *Hold on just a little longer. I'm going to get us out of here.*

The boy placed the scale in the wedge of the grinding stone and the wheel. The monks began to rock back and forth to crush the scale. As soon as enough of the scale had been crushed into a powder, Dorothy nodded to the other monks. They stopped rocking the wheel. As soon as it stopped, Dorothy tried reaching over to grab a handful of the blue powder. One of the guards noticed the monks had stopped rolling the grinding stone.

"Hey! Why did you all stop? Keep grinding."

The monks didn't comply. Dorothy was still trying to reach for the powder, it was only inches away from her grasp. The Tong who yelled out to them began to walk over to them. Dorothy had to grab the powder before he reached them; otherwise her plan would be ruined before it even started. Her heart was racing, and her palms were sweaty. She mustered up all the strength she had in her to press her full weight into the direction of the powder. The iron cuff, that chained her hand to the pushing post began to dig into her wrist, scraping back the top layer of her skin. It was just enough to grab a clutch of powder before the guard approached the group.

"I said, why did you stop? Now push before I decide to feed you to the beast!"

"They stopped, because I have to use the restroom," Dorothy responded.

"Use it on yourself and get back to work."

"And risk it draining into your only source of fresh drinking water?"

Dorothy motioned her head to the slope of the ground under her feet leading to the edge of the plateau into the small lake at the basin of the cavern.

"Fine."

The guard uncuffed Dorothy from the post to lead her back up. Before walking out, the guard peered back over his shoulder at the monks, and they began to rock the stone again over the crushed scale.

Dorothy took her time walking up the tunnel steps making a mental note of the gas lines that traversed the side of the walls and into each side room. At the base of the tunnel was a storage room. Inside was dynamite crates. Dorothy could see that the dynamite was weeping on the side. Above it was a gas lantern with a small copper pipe running to it feeding it from the main line in the tunnel. Dorothy was calculated and poised, like that of spy behind enemy lines.

The guard behind her gave her shove, pushing Dorothy forward up the steps.

"I thought you said you had to go to the bathroom."

Dorothy caught herself with her left hand but scraped her knee. She was still clutching the blue dragon powder in her right hand. Dorothy picked herself up off the floor and proceeded up the tunnel stairs. The small pain throbbing at her knee was miniscule compared to what would await her, if she failed.

The two finally made it to the cell room. Dorothy stopped at the opening. The man pushed her in the back. This time Dorothy stood firm with one had on the stone opening.

"I can't go with you looking. You need to stay out here until I'm done."

The monk grunted with annoyance.

"Hurry up then."

Dorothy went it in. The cell door was open, and the bucket was set over to the corner of the cell. Dorothy didn't have to really go to the bathroom, but she knew if the guard didn't hear the sound hitting the bottom of the pail, he would come in to take her back down. Just then, Dorothy saw the porcelain teapot the gang brewed tea in at breakfast, lunch, and dinner. They had just as much of a fancy for the beverage as her English friend did on the *Hoover.*

Dorothy grabbed the teapot and slowly tipped it over into the pail to insinuate the sound of her relieving herself. As she was pouring the tea, she looked around for the tea tin. It was sitting next to the Mahjong board. She grabbed it with her fisted hand and curled it back into her body. Once she had the tin against her chest, she bent over to open the top of the tin, while being careful to continue to pour the tea into the pail.

The top of the tin popped off and out of her mouth. It sprung up into the air like a loose spring. Dorothy's eyes widened as it fell towards the rocky floor. Her heart skipped a beat as she kicked her leg out to try and catch it with her foot. The tin top bounced off her foot and landed onto a clutter of hay on the ground. It barely made a sound.

She wasn't in the clear yet. Dorothy was running out of tea. The stream began to slow to a drip. Dorothy scattered the blue dragon into the top of the tin and rushed to grab the top off the ground to place everything back as normal.

"Are you done?", the guard asked from outside.

Dorothy rushed to get back into the cell with the pail. She squatted over it as she pulled her pants halfway down just before the guard came from around the corner.

"Hey don't look!", Dorothy shouted.

The guard averted his head to the side, as Dorothy's voice startled him. She stood up to pull her pants back up and

tied her cloth belt tightly around her waist. Every move
Dorothy made was only a split second away from being her
last.

"Let's go.", the man ordered.

Dorothy exited the cell room and began to head back
down the tunnel. She took her time once again, looking into
each side room to get familiar with her surroundings before
her escape back up.

She stopped for a pause right before the last room.
The room with the dynamite. Dorothy knew this would test
the patience of her keeper. Just like she predicted, the guard
shoved Dorothy forward. Dorothy directed her overreacted
fall to the left inside the room. The guard yelled at her to get
up and out of the room.

Dorothy picked herself off of the floor and grabbed
onto the small copper hose feeding the lantern to pick herself
up to her feet. Before pushing back off the wall and back to
the tunnel, Dorothy put her full weight on the hose causing it
to snap at the connection to the lantern. The light flickered as
some of the gas began to escape downward. She paused
hoping the guard didn't realize, what she had done. The guard
didn't notice, though, and pulled Dorothy out of the room and
into the tunnel by the arm before pushing her forward into the
cavern.

The two walked back to the grinding stone, where the other Tongs were unbuckling the monks from the shaft in order to collect the remaining powder. It was nearing lunch time at this point. The cook came down the tunnel with a pot of broth soup for everyone. On top of the pot was the tea pot with the tin and a few cups for the Tongs.

The plan was working. It looked like good fortune was now in Dorothy's favor. The cook set the pot of broth down and served everyone a bowl of ramen. The Tongs had noodles in their bowl. While everyone began to eat, Dorothy watched the cook intently. Her eyes were affixed on every move, like a director would with a film set. The only difference is that Dorothy would only get one take.

The cook went over to the lake to scoop up some fresh water to boil for the tea pot. After the water was warmed, he opened up the tin to mix in the tea leaves. Only instead of tea, the cook scooped up the Blue Dragon powder Dorothy had placed in there just moments before.

Dorothy leaned over to Bodhi, "We must stall being chained back to the post until the powder kicks in."

Bodhi looked back in acknowledgement. All the Tongs began to drink the tea except for the boy with bamboo stick. Just before he could take a sip from his cup, he was ordered to go fetch more hay for the smoke pillow so that they could harvest another scale after lunch. This would put a kink in Dorothy's plan, but she was committed now. She would have to keep with her plan.

The guards got up from their lunch and had finished all their tea at this point. The powder had not yet kicked in. One guard approached the monks and Dorothy to chain them back to the post. Dorothy looked over to Bodhi for help. He looked back to her and said, "Remember to be like water, flow around the obstacles placed before you."

Dorothy began to sweat. *What was she going to do? The powder hadn't kicked in yet.*

"All right, back to your feet.", the one guard demanded.

Bodhi looked up at the guard, "Great leader of the Tong, I ask that you allow me and my brothers to meditate to regain our strength for the remaining day's work. It will only be a few minutes, but we will be able to work much harder, if you would be so kind to grant us this request."

The guard rubbed his head as the powder began to show the first signs of kicking in.

"Very well. You," the guard pointed to Dorothy, "You don't need to mediate. Stand up so I can lock you back in."

Dorothy stood up slowly, trying to buy every second she could get. The guard shoved her over to the post and waited for her to put her hands up in the cuffs. Dorothy didn't comply. He slammed the butt of this handgun in his clutches against the post, while standing right behind her. Dorothy slowly began to raise her arms to the post. She was beginning to give up hope that the plan could be carried out any farther.

Before she could give up, one of the other Tongs began to hallucinate and was entranced by the fire, that had been boiling the pot of water for the tea. He began to sway back and forth, losing his sense of balance. The man fell face-forward into the fire. Sparks flew up into the air like little fireflies. The other Tongs began hallucinating as well and were having difficulty assisting their partner.

The commotion was exactly what Dorothy needed. It turned the guard's attention directly behind her to focus on the others. Dorothy felt this shift of focus behind her. She reared her elbow forward before thrusting it back into the gut of the large man's belly. The force combined with the effects of the blue dragon was enough to cause the man to stumble backwards onto his back. His gun flew across the floor, rattling as the metal skipped off the rock.

Dorothy looked at Bodhi. They both knew this was the moment. This would be goodbye. Dorothy darted for the gun before the man could regain himself. She snatched it off the ground as she ran for the rocky stalagmite bridge connected to her one way out, the entrance to the tunnel.

The other guards finally got the commotion under control and noticed Dorothy making a run for the entrance. They all started to shout orders at one another in attempt to regain some type of control over the situation. As the Tongs began to pursue Dorothy, she was already halfway down the bridge. She grabbed one of the torches that lit the cavern as she was running out.

Dorothy made it to the cavern entrance and up the first few steps. She stopped at the side room where the dynamite was being stored. She turned back around and saw the monks kneeling around the head of the dragon with their hands placed on its head. They looked to be chanting some sort of healing prayer. Then her eyes were brought down to see the Tong men running towards her.

Dorothy took a deep breath before tossing the torch in the room with the dynamite. She turned around and began running up the tunnel stairs as fast as she could. The other Tongs were in hot pursuit.

Right before they made it to the tunnel entrance; the torch Dorothy had tossed, slowly rolled in front, to the stream of gas spewing from the lantern's lines. It ignited. The fire carried up the stream of gas like dragon's breath. Within fractions of a second, the dynamite was ignited, blowing the rock around the room to bits. The blast was enough to knock every Tong and Dorothy to the ground.

Before the shock wave of the blast cleared all the way up the tunnel, the entrance to the cavern began to cave in. The stalactites began falling from the ceiling of the cavern, crushing the Tongs below. The dragon and the monks were untouched. Instead the crack in the ceiling, where the waterfall poured out broke away. A path to the surface was made. The universe was in favor of the mystical creature.

All this was unknown to Dorothy, who began running back up the seven hundred and ninety-three steps to her freedom after recovering from the blast. She was covered in rock dust that had traveled up with the shock wave. The tunnel was beginning to collapse.

As she was running up the tunnel, she ran into the boy with the bamboo stick. They were both surprised to see the other. He swung his stick at Dorothy's head. She ducked. The stick just missed her. The swing opened a path for Dorothy to run past him to the right. She darted by and ran up the steps.

Before she could get too far, the boy reached for a handgun he had tucked into his waist band after the blast. He began to pop off rounds. Each one missed Dorothy, but they were getting closer and closer to hitting her. The tunnel had a straightaway. She wasn't going to be able to outrun the gunfire. Dorothy saw a side room just above, to the right. She dove in to take cover.

The tunnel was shaking from the collapsing rock. Dorothy had her back against the wall with the handgun firmly in both her hands positioned up in the crevasse of her chest. She was breathing heavily. Before she spun out to return fire, she saw her camera hanging on the post of the bed of one of the Tong members. She grabbed it and threw it around her neck.

Dorothy took two more deep breaths to focus. She spun out and aimed the gun at the boy and squeezed the trigger twice. The last shot hit the boy in the shoulder. He fired his gun as he fell backwards down the stairs. The sound echoed loudly in the tunnel chamber. Dorothy felt a burst of pressure against her gut like she was hit by a truck. She didn't have time to check, if she had been shot. The tunnel had begun to collapse.

Dorothy made it up the rest of the tunnel just before it collapsed all the way. She made her way through the monastery to look and see if the truck had arrived with its shipment. It was parked in the courtyard. The driver had already gotten out and begun to unlatch the back to unload the truck.

The collapse of the tunnel and gunfire must have not been heard by the driver. He was older and his hearing must have been starting to go. Dorothy was going to use this to her advantage to try to steal the truck, when the old man wasn't looking.

The nearest city that Dorothy knew of was Shanghai; and that was from what she remembered a three to four-hour drive from the monastery. Dorothy squatted down behind the ornate railing wrapping around the porch of the courtyard. As she was directly across from the driver-side door, Dorothy looked to see if the old man was still back behind the truck. She couldn't see him. *This is it.* She thought to herself.

Dorothy sprung up and jumped over the railing using the last bit of energy she had to make a mad dash for the truck. She hopped in the cab and popped the clutch. The truck began to roll forward, alerting the old man that his truck was being stolen. The old man came around to the driver side to find Dorothy looking desperately for the gear shift to put it in drive.

The man reached up to the handle to open the door. Dorothy grabbed the inside handle to slam it back shut. The old man fell backward, and Dorothy shifted the truck into gear. She pressed the gas pedal and drove out the monastery's front gate. She was free. She escaped. The relief of freedom was short lived as she went to grab her lower abdomen, where the one boy had shot at her. It was pounding with pain, now that the adrenaline from her escape had begun to settle.

SHANGHAI HIDEAWAY

Issue 16

Dorothy pulled her blouse up out of her pants. She moved her hand across her stomach to check for an entry wound. She couldn't feel any. There was no blood either. She breathed in a deep breath and then winced at the pain. She definitely had a broken rib. Dorothy took the camera off from around her neck to give her lungs some room to breathe.

As she set it to the side, the glass from the lens fell out onto the bench seat. Dorothy picked the camera back up to look inside the lens. Only fragments of glass remained around the rim of the removable lens. Inside she could see a compressed lead bullet jingling around from the bumpy road. Dorothy tipped the camera over dropping the bullet into her other hand. She rolled the bullet back and forth between her fingers as she drove down the country road thinking about how lucky she was that the bullet had hit the camera.

About three hours into her journey, Dorothy looked down at the dirty fuel gauge in the dash. It was nearing empty again just as she was coming to a fork in the road. She pulled the truck over and went to the back to fetch the gas can and the funnel. The sign at the road said Shanghai: 8 miles with an arrow pointing to the right.

Before Dorothy could finish emptying the can into the tank, a farmer came around the bend. He was driving a cart with his wife. The cart was being pulled by an old ox. In the back looked to be the couple's rice harvest. They were headed to Shanghai to sell their crop at the market.

Dorothy waved the couple down. She knew the Tong Gang was crawling all over Shanghai. She would get scooped right back up if she rolled back into the city on their stolen truck.

"Excuse me."

The man pulled back on the reins of the ox, and the cart came to a stop. Dorothy asked them, if they were going to Shanghai. They were.

"Would you mind giving me a lift into the city?" Dorothy asked.

"What's the matter? Is your truck broken?", the farmer asked.

"No."

The farmer's wife leaned over to her husband. "Come on let's go. She's crazy."

The farmer replied back to Dorothy, "Well it looks like our Ox can only pull two of us with our harvest in tow. I'm very sorry."

"Take the truck then. You can have it. The other can take me into the city."

The farmer leaned back over to his wife shocked at the offer. "What do I say now?"

The wife replied, "Take the truck, are you crazy?" The wife kicked her husband off the cart and motioned for Dorothy to hop in the cart next to her. When Dorothy passed the farmer, she said, "The keys are in the ignition." The farmer bowed and smiled as he passed her by.

Dorothy got up in the cart, with her broken camera hanging around her neck. The farmer's wife caught a glimpse of this and stared forward deciding not to talk to her on the way in. The woman thought Dorothy was certified crazy.

Giving away a perfectly good truck but holding onto a broken camera.

After a four-hour, awkwardly silent ride, the two made it into the city. Dorothy thanked her for the ride. It was nighttime at this point. The first thing Dorothy had to do was get her belongings back from the Fairmont Peace hotel.

When Dorothy walked into the hotel, she was not greeted with the same enthusiasm she had been granted before. Then again, given her rough and dirty appearance, who could blame them.

"Madam, beggars are not welcome here."

"No, sir, you misunderstand. I am only here to collect my things."

"What things?"

"My bag sir. The name's Dorothy Summers. I stayed here a little over a week ago, in room 306."

The man gave Dorothy a doubtful look before reaching for the ledger beneath the desks. The man flipped a few pages back. "Ah yes, Dorothy Summers. It says right here that you failed to check out."

"Let's say, that I ran into some rotten luck, that prevented me from doing so."

"Err. Uh huh. Well then."

The man rang the bell on his desk. The bell hop that had helped Dorothy with her bag when she first checked in approached the front desk.

"Please fetch. Ms. Summer's belongings from the storage room next to the boiler."

The boy hurried off to make quick work of the clerk's request. The boy returned with her bag before the clerk could refile last week's ledger back underneath the desk.

"Thank you."

Dorothy grabbed the bag from the boy, and opened it to search it for her journal, where she had written the story down the night before she was abducted by the Tongs.

"It's not here."

"What's not there?", the clerk asked.

"My journal, it must still be in the nightstand. You must let me go back up to retrieve it."

"Unfortunately, there is nothing I can do for you at the moment. Room 306 is currently occupied. If you will return between the hours of eleven and three, you can search the room for your journal after the guest has checked out."

Frustrated, tired, and hurt. Dorothy didn't want to cause a commotion, so she left the lobby of the hotel. The only problem was that the remainder of Dorothy's money was kept between the pages of her journal. She wouldn't have anything to book her accommodations for the night.

Dorothy began to walk down the streets of Shanghai. She was looking for a cozy shop nook where she could get some shut eye until the morning. As she was looking to the side, she ran into a man. It was the docker who had set her up by the docks. Dorothy knew immediately who he was. Her face struck a sense of familiarity with the man, when he looked down to see who had bumped into him.

Dorothy apologized in Mandarin and tucked her head as she walked around him. The docker went back to taunting the shop owner he was tasked to collect protection money from. Before the docker could take a second glance back up to get a look at Dorothy, she had already slipped past the crowd and tucked herself into the dark alleyway.

Dorothy found a pile of garbage to hide behind. She wasn't going to risk getting caught by the Tong Gang again. She tried her hardest to get some rest, but the stench of the foul pile of trash next to her made it impossible. Still, it was better than having to sleep one more night in the cell at the monastery.

The next morning, Dorothy made her way back to the hotel to collect her journal. When the clerk from the night before smelled Dorothy, he told her that Bao the bellhop would escort her to room 306 through the service elevator. He didn't want her disturbing the guests.

Bao opened the door to her old hotel room and waited for Dorothy to enter. He stood at the entrance as Dorothy made it over to the nightstand where she had kept her journal. It was still there. She opened it up, and there was the cash. All wasn't lost. Dorothy handed Bao one of the gold units as a tip for his help. Before heading back down, Dorothy asked Bao, if he knew of any place where she could stay for an extended time for a bargain.

Bao told her of a young lady near his neighborhood who rented out cheap room and board to some Russian refugees who had come to Shanghai after their revolution. Dorothy tipped the boy another gold unit and thanked him again before heading to the Honkew district.

Once Dorothy arrived, she asked around for a Pan Yuliang. Two women at a bathhouse pointed her to some old looking run-down apartments. Dorothy smiled. This was the perfect place to hideaway until she finished her story.

THE JOURNALIST, THE PAINTER, AND THE DANCER

Issue 17

Dorothy approached the apartment building. It was a wooden building that looked like the old-style Chinese architecture she was used to in San Francisco. The rest of the city was sprawling with the new art-deco style. Shanghai was beginning to experience a golden age. This spot, the district, and the building were an exception, still untouched by the economic renaissance that covered the rest of the city.

There was a gate entrance in the middle of the building with a wooden door opened in the left gate. Dorothy stepped over the tall threshold of the inlayed door. A woman was sitting in an apartment to the left. The window was open, and she was painting in her living and dining area. Dorothy asked her where Pan was, only to find out that the woman painting was Pan.

"I'm looking for a place to stay and heard that you might have some room available."

"Yes, we have a bed available. You would have to share the room though."

"That's fine. I'll only be staying her for a few weeks."

The *S.S. Hoover* wouldn't return to Shanghai for another two and a half weeks. That would be enough time for Dorothy to finish her story and lay low from the Tongs. Pan could smell Dorothy through her window and became suspicious of her ability to cover the rent.

"You will have to pay in advance."

"That won't be a problem."

Dorothy reached into her bag to pull out her journal. She opened it up to the middle to pull out her cash. Dorothy handed over two weeks' worth of rent. She figured the math from the rate per day sign next to the door on the gate. Pan saw the journal.

"Are you a writer?"

"I'm a journalist. I'm currently working on a story for my uncle's magazine."

"In that case, you can get the artist's discount."

Pan split the cash units in half and handed the other stack back over to Dorothy. Dorothy didn't see how investigative journalism was art, but she wasn't about to argue with her. Maybe the lady took pity on Dorothy due to her foul smell and look.

Pan grabbed a key off the wall next to her canvas, then proceeded to walk out. She motioned for Dorothy to follow her. The apartment building was open to a square courtyard in the middle with a few tables and chairs set up for people to gather in the open air. No one was outside at this time besides an older lady practicing her late morning Tai Chi.

The two walked up a rickety wooden staircase to a wraparound balcony. The apartment she was taking Dorothy to was only two doors down. Pan told her that her roommate was not in right now, and that she worked the night shift but should be arriving soon. Pan mentioned that she was Russian. Dorothy didn't seem to care much either way as long as she wasn't Tong.

Pan opened the door to the unit. Inside were two twin iron beds with a thin mattress and a blanket. A single nightstand was between them with a gas lantern sitting on top. A dresser was by the door with a small mirror hung above. To the other corner was a wooden bathtub, almost like a large wooden pail. Next to the tub was a small pail.

"You can use the handpump in the courtyard to draw your bath. The bathroom is downstairs next to the corner unit. You can use the amenities in the courtyard to wash your clothes or for cooking."

Dorothy looked out the door through the balcony railing to see a circle stone wash basin and a stone fire pit with some food-encrusted black woks hanging on a rack next to it. She was used to not having access to the most modern of amenities, but this was a little less than she was used to. It didn't matter though; comfort wasn't what she was needing in a place. The seclusion was enough for her.

Dorothy set her stuff on the bed and took the unit key from Pan. She laid out her fresh change of clothes and grabbed the pail in the corner to go draw her bath. Dorothy began pumping the water and making her trips up to the room. On her twelfth trip, she saw a beautiful woman come through the gate with long blond hair. She was tall and lean, but fit. She walked up the stairs and entered Dorothy's room. This must have been the Russian roommate Pan had told her about.

After filing up the pail, Dorothy went to her unit to dump it out into the tub. She walked in on the Russian looking at her stuff.

"I see I have a new roommate."

"The name's Dorothy."

"Nice to meet you Dorothy. I'm Yelena. I'm sure well have more time to catch up later. However, I just got back from a night shift, so I'll be turning in now."

"I heard. Pan told me about it. Not to worry, I won't be a bother."

Yelena gave a soft but tired smile before pulling the blanket off her bed to lie down for sleep. Dorothy looked down to a barely half-filled tub. She didn't want to disturb her roommate who was surprisingly already asleep by filling up the tub with any more trips. She set the pail down and retrieved her bar of soap from the bag. She then undressed and quietly lapped the water over her body trying to scrub the week and a half of filth off of her.

After her bath, Dorothy changed into her set of fresh clothes. She felt like royalty, ironically. The fresh feeling rejuvenated her. Dorothy grabbed her dirty clothes and journal and went down to the courtyard. She figured she would give Yelena some peace and quiet.

Dorothy hung her hand-washed clothes over the balcony railing before returning back down to the courtyard. She set-up at one of the tables and began to write in her journal. She picked back up by writing about the encounter late at night when she was tied to the chair at the warehouse.

Three hours must have passed since Dorothy had last sat down. She had gotten into a zone while writing. She almost didn't notice Pan, who had just emerged from her apartment. She had a pot of tea and two cups with her. Dorothy looked up to acknowledge her just as she sat the pot down at the table.

"Would you like some tea?", Pan offered.

"Yes, that would be nice."

"I see you are busy writing away. What is your story about?"

Dorothy told Pan the story about the Tongs, the Blue Dragon drug trade, and how she had been kidnapped and taken to the mountain side. The only thing Dorothy left out was the dragon itself. Dorothy didn't know why. Maybe she didn't think Pan would take her or the rest of her story seriously, if she had.

Pan then shared with Dorothy that she had only recently come back from Paris where she had studied Western-style painting. She was running the apartment for her great Aunt in exchange for free board. She used the opportunity to focus on her paintings. Pan reminded Dorothy a lot of her father. Just speaking with her made Dorothy realize how much she missed her family, even crazy Uncle Shu.

The two talked for a while. The tea in Dorothy's cup ran cold before she could finish it. Eventually, Yelena emerged from the apartment after sleeping through lunch. She joined the other two at table.

"Ah Yelena, how was work last night?" Pan inquired.

"The usual: old, ugly men barking like dogs."

Pan told Dorothy about the dance hall Yelena worked at as a hostess. She also described the men in Shanghai.

"Even though Shanghai has progressed, the men have not."

Yelena gives a laugh.

"Were they the same back in Russia?" Dorothy asked.

"I'm not sure. I was only a little girl when I was last there. My family fled after the revolution in 1917. Although, you know what they say, 'You can polish a piece of shit until it shines, but it will never be a Fabergé.' If a man is a dog inside, it doesn't matter how well he dresses on the outside. He will still behave as a dog."

"Yelena was an aristocrat," Pan explained.

"Yes, it is true. I lived in a mansion, wore beautiful dresses, and ate caviar. All gone now. I have to actually work for a living, now that my father has passed."

"Why don't you work at a place doing what you love?"

"Well it's not that simple. The only things I know how to do are look pretty and dance ballet."

"Why not make a living dancing ballet at one of the theaters here in the city?"

"I don't know if that's possible."

"I thought the same thing, until my father encouraged me to do otherwise. He's one of the good men, with a heart as beautiful as a Fabergé. My old boss: not so much. It was he that first suggested I go work for my Uncle. That's why I'm here now."

This piqued Yelena's interest. Dorothy retold the same story to Yelena that she had previously told Pan. The only difference was that this time, Yelena asked why they called the powder Blue Dragon.

Dorothy responded to Yelena's question after hesitation, "It is going to be hard to believe, because I didn't believe it myself until I saw it with my own eyes. The drug comes from the scales of a real dragon."

It was silent. The other two looked at each other and then back at Dorothy before Yelena busted out in laughter.

"You are right about one thing. I won't believe it until I see it with my eyes. You are a creative one."

Dorothy sunk in her seat. She now knew how Uncle Shu felt. Except for Shu, the disbelief from others seemed to roll off him like water on a duck feather. For Dorothy the disbelief hit her harder than the lead bullet.

She began to wish the Tongs didn't take her roll of film away. If she had a picture of the dragon, she would be able to prove her story true. It would go from a fictional fantasy tale to an investigative headline piece that would shock the world. But alas, it was too late. As adventurous and courageous as Dorothy was, she was not about to journey back to the monastery for a photo.

"We're only joking around with you Dorothy. That is a very intriguing story. We are sure others would enjoy reading it," Yelena reassured her.

Unfortunately, it wasn't very reassuring. How would Dorothy sell this story. She had come too far for it to collect dust like some of Shu's magazine issues.

Dorothy decided to go up to her room for some rest. When she sat on the bed, she stared at the broken camera. It was symbolic of her crushed hope. The flame for journalism was dying down to just a flicker. She picked the camera to rub its edges as she thought about everything she had gone through in the past month.

Her thumb rubbed across the film cassette toggle at the top as she rubbed the side of the case. Dorothy felt some resistance to it. She sat up straight on the bed. *Could it be?* Dorothy quickly rolled the toggle all the way before opening the back of the camera. Inside to her disbelief, was a cartridge of full film.

Fortune was once again favoring Dorothy. One of the Tongs must have replaced the film cartridge after they took her camera. *Could a picture of the dragon exist on the film?* She had to find out. She needed to get the roll developed.

Later that night, Dorothy would turn her apartment into a dark room in order to develop the roll of film. After she processed the film in the solution, she hung the blank photographic paper up on the wall above the side of her bed. Dorothy sat on Yelena's bed just staring at the string of photos. She waited intently for the images to appear. Then it happened. The middle photo began to appear. There it was. The answer to Dorothy's question. The one thing that changed her story from folklore to a reputable piece of journalism. Dorothy stared at a photo of the Tong gang lined up in front of the Blue Dragon. The world was about to change forever.

FIRST EDITION

Issue 18

Two weeks had come and gone in the blink of an eye. Dorothy had finally finished her story. From the *Chronicle* to the dragon. She hadn't told her new friends about the picture still. She didn't want to bring too much attention to herself until the story was published. They would find out anyway. Dorothy had planned on sending a copy of the magazine to the apartments after Wang Shu finished publishing it.

Dorothy had rewritten the story on clean parchment in a more legible form. She wanted to make sure there was no confusion, when Uncle received it. The photo was tucked between the papers. She didn't want anyone to accidently see it on her way to the post office.

The post office was bustling with all kinds of traffic. Dorothy had to wait in line before she was called up to the front clerk. While standing there, Dorothy surveyed all the people going in and out of the store. People of all backgrounds and cultures going about their day. Most of them clueless to what laid outside of town just a four-hour drive away. Here she was in the middle of the fifth-largest city in the world, about to send the biggest story ever halfway back across the globe to sell a few hundred first edition copies.

That moment an English gentleman walked into the store behind Dorothy. He reminded her of her friend from the *Hoover.* The British publisher. She then remembered the note with his office's address.

Dorothy turned around to the gentleman. "Excuse me sir, but do you mind if I borrow your ink pen for just a moment?"

The gentleman obliged, and Dorothy pulled out the paper with the publisher's address. At the top she wrote: "Send a copy of the first edition to this address. Mark it with 'From Dorothy, your dinner guest from the *Hoover.*'"

Dorothy returned the pen back to the nice gentleman before she was called up to the front of the line.

"Next!"

Dorothy went up to the stall.

"I need a first-class air mail package to San Francisco"

The clerk exchanged the package and the stamps. Dorothy slid the story and letter to her uncle into the package and wrote Wang Shu's address on it before handing it back over. She felt a weight lift off of her. Now it was in the hands of her uncle. The world would decide if Dorothy's courage held value to them. Would the story make the impact, she had hoped for? Time would tell. All she knew, is that she completed it. She finished what she set out to do and stayed true to herself.

Dorothy went on to board the *Hoover* the next day. It would be two weeks before she was back in San Francisco. By that time, the letter would have already arrived at Wang Shu's Magazine. Dorothy was hoping Uncle would be nearing completion on the story in editing by the time she had arrived.

Little did Dorothy know that the story she had written would spark a fire inside her uncle. A few days after the story was sent out, it was delivered to her uncle by a courier. Wang Shu knew immediately that it was from Dorothy. He began to open the package at the bottom of his steep stairs.

Shu slid the papers out and read Dorothy's letter as he began walking up the stairs. After reading the letter, he flipped through the pages one by one giving them a quick glance. Then as he flipped the next page, only one step from the top; Wang Shu revealed the photo of the dragon.

He grabbed the side of the wall and paused. Moment after moment passed as he stared the picture over. Emotions were turning over inside of Dorothy's uncle. Never has anyone of his stories ever been accompanied with photographic proof. Wang Shu knew things were about to change.

He pushed off the wall, rushed to his desk, and began to set up the press. Old Shu worked tirelessly without break, almost sixteen hours straight. The hard work paid off. Only four days after the pages left Dorothy's fingertips, the story that was first started by a piece of cloth in the mailroom was now bound in a Wang Shu First Edition print copy.

Shu cackled as he held up the first print off the press. "Mystery of the Blue Dragon," by Dorothy Summers. He continued printing copies until he ran out of ink.

The next day Wang Shu took the first bundle from his shop and set out to distribute them. His first stop would be Hank's. As Shu approached the door to the dress store, Hank saw him through the bay window as he was redressing the mannequin. Hank smiled and stepped back from the window to let Shu in.

"Mr. Shu, my goodness this is a surprise. I wanted to thank you for the last issue Dorothy sent me. My nephew was elated to read the story. Such a vivid imagination. Where do you come up with your tales?"

"Oh Hank, I am not the creative type, I assure you. I also know that you don't have a nephew."

Hank's smile turned down a little, "I guess I'm used to hiding the things I like."

Wang Shu patted Hank on the back as he walked over to his counter. Hank followed and stood across from Shu. Shu put the stack of magazines up on the counter so that he could pull out a single copy from the inside of his tattered coat pocket.

"Maybe it's time you stop hiding the things that bring you happiness. I'm counting on you to share my niece's story with everyone you know."

Wang Shu handed Hank the copy. Hank opened the magazine up. On the first page was a picture of the dragon. Hank's eyes widened.

"Is this real?"

"As real as you and me."

"Then your stories. Are they all real?"

Shu smiled as he grabbed the stack of magazines off the counter.

"I hope you enjoy the story Hank."

Wang Shu left Hank at the counter, glued to the magazine he had just dropped off. Next, he would take the copies from store to store and then to his subscriber's homes.

Word of the *Mystery of the Blue Dragon* spread throughout the hilly streets of San Francisco faster than Wang Shu could print copies. Hank had told every mistress, gossiping housewife, daughter, and young woman that entered his store about Dorothy Summer's story.

Wang Shu knew his press could not keep up with his readers. He decided to take copy to the post office, where he mailed a first edition of *Mystery of the Blue Dragon* to the British publisher.

The package arrived in London at the office of the publisher Dorothy had befriended on the *Hoover*. It was intercepted by the man's secretary.

"Virgil sir, there's a package that's been delivered to you. It looks urgent."

Virgil huffed, "Well give it here then. We mustn't waste any time getting to it shall we?"

When Virgil opened the package, a small letter fell out. It read, "From Dorothy, your dinner guest from the *Hoover.*" Virgil then pulled a copy of the magazine out. He read it cover to cover without hesitation.

Without saying a word. Virgil got up from his desk to go to his print team a few offices down. He barged through the door and slammed the magazine on top of the lead's desks.

"I want a second edition of this magazine sent out to every single publishing office we have around the world."

The woman picked the magazine off her desk. She looked back up at Virgil.

"What is this?"

"The next Verne."

Mystery of the Blue Dragon would be printed and distributed across the British Empire. Every British citizen and colonist would come to know or hear of the name Dorothy Summers almost as much as their dear King George V.

Dorothy couldn't imagine the ripple affect her story would have on the world. She would first learn of its impact on the city of San Francisco when she returned from Shanghai.

A STAR BEHIND BARS

Issue 19

Two weeks felt like two months. Dorothy's journey on the *Hoover* back to San Francisco didn't feel as exciting as the journey to Shanghai. She was grateful to be going back home. The stagnation of sitting on a boat without going back to a thrilling chase for another story loomed over Dorothy's head like a dark cloud. The forecast was about to clear up though. The *Hoover* would port in the Bay Area first thing in the morning.

As the sun rose over the bay, the crowds lined up to watch an unsuspecting Dorothy deboard the ship. Unbeknownst to Dorothy, all of San Francisco had already read about her journey in the *Mystery of the Blue Dragon*.

She began to make her way down the gangway. There was shouting at the bottom. Dorothy could see a man nuzzle his way to the front of the crowd. It was Ollie from the *Chronicle. What was he doing there?* Dorothy thought to herself.

FLASH. Ollie's camera went off right in Dorothy's face.

"Say Dorothy, how did you escape the Tong Gang in Shanghai? Is the dragon still alive? Do you have a follow-up story lined up?"

The questions coming from Ollie were whizzed at Dorothy so quickly, she didn't have time to respond.

"What do you mean? Who told you about these things?"

"Are you telling me the story's a fraud. Another off-the-wall spoof of your uncle's?"

"What? No? I'm really not in a place to be talking about this right now."

Ollie began jotting down Dorothy's responses with his pencil as she began to push past him through the crowd. Once she got to the other side, her uncle was waiting in his truck.

"Oh Uncle, am I glad to see you. Did you get my story?"

"Indeed, I did. We have a lot to talk about."

Uncle Shu grabbed Dorothy's bag and tossed it in the back. The two got in the truck to push past the rest of the crowd. On the drive back to Chinatown, Shu revealed to Dorothy that he had already put the story to print. He gave her a copy of the first edition issue to her for her to read in the car.

The magazine turned out great. There were a few Chinatown business ads scattered in the back, but the majority of the issue was practically Dorothy's story.

"You did good little one," Shu commented as he smiled while focusing on the road ahead. "I'm going to need your help at the press. The copies are selling faster than I can make them. The whole town's talking about it. Not just Chinatown either. All of San Francisco. Isn't that wonderful?"

Dorothy looked at her uncle and then back down at her magazine. She couldn't believe it. All she had worked so hard for, finally realized. She was a journalist, a well-known one at that.

The next day Dorothy got to work with Shu loading paper into the press to run more copies of the issue. After they printed enough for a bundle, Shu sent Dorothy off to make some runs to restock the magazine around town. As she exited Chinatown, everyone on the sidewalks with a newspaper was staring at Dorothy.

One woman jeered at her, telling Dorothy that she was a fake. A man sitting down at a trolley bench looked out from his paper to tell her that she should have stayed in the mail room. Dorothy's blood began to boil like it used to whenever Arthur Henry would make some sexist remark to her at her old job.

Dorothy finally made it to the general store to drop off the stack of magazines with Elmo, the store's owner.

"You doin' alright there, Dorothy.", Elmo asked.

"Just some jerks on the street. I'll be fine though."

"Ignore them, some people just believe everything they read."

Dorothy's face looked confused. "What are you talking about?" she asked.

"The paper this morning. The *Chronicle* did a little exposé piece on you and your dragon story. They really did a numba on ya."

"Let me see that."

Dorothy reached to grab the paper right out of Elmo's hands. She read the headline on the front page. If she wasn't mad before, she would be now. It read, "Dorothy Summers: Journalist or Fraud?"

Ollie had taken his interview with Dorothy and twisted it to make her look like she fabricated the whole story about the blue dragon. She took Elmo's paper and headed right out the door without saying another word. Uncle had to hear about the slander the *Chronicle* had written about them.

Upon returning to Wang Shu's Monster Magazine, Dorothy found a cop and a police detective waiting for her outside of the almond cookie shop. They approached her to stop her from going inside.

"Miss, are you Dorothy Summers?"

"I am. Why do you ask?"

The one cop looked to the detective. The detective answered, "We'd like for you to come down to the station with us. We have some questions about your story on the Blue Dragon."

It wasn't like Dorothy was going to refuse a request from a big city detective, so she went with them downtown to the station. On the way in, Dorothy could only think to herself.

Great. Just as fortune shined on me, a bunch of dirty buffoons at the Chronicle *come a long to unravel it all.*

Dorothy was escorted to the detective's desk. She sat across from the detective while the other cop leaned up against the desk with his forearm on his leg. The cop did all the talking, while the detective observed how Dorothy answered.

"So is your story true or not?"

"Of course it's true. Every word of it. I have journalistic integrity, you know."

"Well then, what do you make of this?"

The cop slapped the newspaper in front of Dorothy. It was the *Chronicle* article that had called Dorothy a fraud.

"I'd say that's a prime example of Arthur Henry throwing a tantrum for me exposing who he really is. I used to work at the *Chronicle*, you know."

The detective piped in before the cop could respond.

"You're saying the whole story is true, every last word of it?"

Dorothy could tell, the two couldn't believe the part about the dragon. Regardless of the photographic evidence in the centerfold of the article.

"Yes. Even, if you don't believe in dragons. You better believe the rest of it. I lived every single page. Almost lost my life chasing down the story."

The detective, then went on to question her about the Blind Tiger Party that she had attended at Mr. Henry's estate. Dorothy gave her statement. She made sure that she didn't implicate herself.

After getting everything they needed to know, they escorted Dorothy to the front of the station. She was walking ahead of them. She knew her way out. It wasn't a hard building to navigate. The other two must have not wanted Dorothy to go snooping through the building. Cops didn't trust journalists in San Francisco at the time. It was no wonder why, given their relationship with Mr. Henry.

The group neared front doors in the hallway of the Police Headquarters. Dorothy heard the cop whispering to the detective.

"We'll never be able to use her testimony against Arthur. His lawyer will get it thrown out on the account of the credibility of the dragon, if we reference her magazine."

Before the detective could give his opinion on the matter, Dorothy opened the front door to the headquarters to exit. As she was met with the bright light on the sunshine, three shots rang out.

The sound of the cracks made Dorothy jump and caused her to fall backwards. No matter how many times she was shot at, Dorothy would never get used to having bullets whiz past or at her through the air.

As soon as Dorothy hit the ground, the cop dragged her back into the building. The detective drew his gun as he slammed the front door shut. He went over to the window to return fire. BANG, BANG, BANG!

The cop frantically tried to get a handle of the situation. He was looking for a gunshot wound on Dorothy's body. There were none. All of the bullets were caught in the wood of the door.

"Did you get him, Clarence?", the cop yelled out. He was still tending to Dorothy, who was lying on her back on the floor in shock.

"No. It was a Tong. He got away."

Dorothy raised her head to address the cop. "Still believe my story isn't credible?"

The next day, a judge put out a warrant for the arrest of Arthur Henry after the presentation of Dorothy's testimony.

A team of cops led by the detective took Arthur Henry into custody at the *Chronicle*.

The whole ordeal hit the headlines the next day. Ollie, the same slime ball that had slandered Dorothy's name, also got a picture of Mr. Henry in cuffs being led out of his office. Edward, a young man with a gimpy leg and a cane, rose to the top as chief editor at the *Chronicle* in the wake of Arthur Henry's arrest. Many of Henry's protégés were skipped over, since the paper thought they could be implicated in Arthur's case.

The cops were still chasing down the Tong who had shot at Dorothy. Getting to see the headline of Mr. Henry in cuffs on the front page was a good distraction to get her mind off the imminent doom she faced with the Tongs. They knew that she had been the cause for their loss of supply to the blue dragon powder and were going to get reparations in the form of her life.

It would be hard for them to get to her, though. She was a celebrity in Chinatown now. The residents who once allowed the Tongs to operate unnoticed in their neighborhood, were now standing up against them after reading Dorothy's story. It made it nearly impossible for the Tongs to get close to Dorothy now.

As Dorothy was making her way to Uncle's after breakfast the next day, she was stopped by Edward. He waddled through the crowd like a penguin, using his cane to push his body sideways to intercept Dorothy.

"Dorothy. Dorothy."

Dorothy looked up and approached Edward so that he didn't have to exert too much more effort getting to her.

"Hello Eddie. Congratulations on your promotion."

"Thank you. That's actually why I'm here. A few of the other journalists left the *Chronicle* after Arthur's arrest, and I was wondering if you would be interested in coming back to work for us. This time as a journalist."

Edward had just offered Dorothy the very position at the same company she dreamt of having just months ago. However, Dorothy was no longer the same person.

Her journey had changed her. She no longer felt like working for the *Chronicle* was her dream. She had lived it working at her uncle's. She didn't want to give that up.

She was glad to see someone like Edward in charge over at the *Chronicle* now. He was a good man. Many of the other after shave, chain-smoking drones of Henry's were rotten apples from the same tree. Not Edward though.

"I really appreciate the offer Eddie, but I think I belong here at my uncle's. As silly as it sounds, *Wang Shu's Monster Magazine* gives me the best opportunity to be who I was meant to be."

"Who is that?"

"Dorothy Summers of course."

Edward smiled. He could see that she was confident in who she was. He tipped his hat to her and wished her good luck, and that he was looking forward to reading her next story.

PECULIAR PROSPERITY

Issue 20

A few months had passed since the first publication of the *Mystery of the Blue Dragon*. Wang Shu and Dorothy were busy printing away copies of the magazine. It was still flying off the shelf. Everyone in San Francisco already had a copy of the magazine. It was the rest of the country that was buying up the articles.

The wealthy in the city were making orders in the hundreds, and then shipping them to bigger cities to turn a profit. Chinatown was on the map for most Americans, thanks to Dorothy Summers.

Dorothy and Wang Shu were working tirelessly making prints all day long. After feeding another ream of paper into the press, Dorothy wiped the sweat dripping down off her brow.

"We are going to need to expand our operations. We won't have any time to chase down the next story if we have to spend all our time printing."

Right at that time, the two heard a ring at the door. A mailman had pulled the string connected to a small bell hanging beside the door. Dorothy got up from the press to go answer the door. The mail man handed Dorothy an envelope. It was addressed to Wang Shu. On the return address was the name Virgil with the address of the British publisher from the *Hoover.*

"Uncle!" Dorothy called.

Her uncle came over to her.

"It's from the publisher."

Dorothy rubbed the back flap of the envelope with her thumb until it wedged itself underneath a loose edge. She then slid her thumb back the other way opening the envelope. Inside was a letter. Dorothy pulled the folded letter out and opened it up to read it.

Sitting in the middle of the letter was a check. It was made out to *Wang Shu's Monster Magazine* in the amount of one hundred fifty-two thousand dollars and zero cents. Dorothy's uncle began to feel lightheaded after reading the amount on the check. He stumbled backwards onto his stool.

Enthusiastic to read what Virgil had to say, Dorothy pinched the check between her ring and pinky finger to hold it behind the letter. She began to read the letter out loud so that old Shu could hear.

"Dear Mr. Shu and Ms. Summers,

I am elated to bring the good news of your magazine's success in our publication of its second edition. I myself was whisked away into the adventure, like Otto Lidenbrock in *Journey to the Center of the Earth.* You have quite a talent, young Dorothy Summers.

In this letter, I have enclosed your royalties to the over five million copies sold throughout the greater commonwealth of the British Empire. I trust you will find its value substantial. Spend it wisely.

Yours Sincerely,

Sir Virgil Butterworth"

Five million copies sold worldwide? The royalties from this would allow them to expand their operations in San Francisco.

"Well Mr. Shu. What do you say to an upgrade?"

"I say time's a wastin'."

The two went to get a commercial relator. They were ready to really branch out and become a major magazine publication. They weren't just going to sell in San Francisco either. They had plans to distribute all across the forty-eight states.

The realtor must have taken Dorothy and Shu to see half a dozen perfectly good facilities for their new magazine, but with each one either Shu or Dorothy would point out a non-negotiable flaw with the place. It did not have anything to do with the space, though. The three didn't find that out till later, when the realtor asked them what they were really looking for. Both knew that the magazine had to stay in Chinatown.

Eventually Dorothy and her uncle decided to put in an offer on two floors of office space directly across from the Shanghai Low night club. The first item they bought after moving in would be a modern German printing press.

They were able to get one that was being sold by a German newspaper for a steal. The owner told Wang Shu, that his business was going bankrupt due to pressure from the new Chancellor that had been elected. Shu couldn't figure out how an election could cause a newspaper to go out of business. Their misfortune would be the magazine's fortune.

The savings allowed them to hire on new staff.
Dorothy decided to hire Ying to help manage distributions.
Next was Dorothy's dad, whom they hired to paint cover art
for their next issues. Dorothy's mom was also hired to manage
the mail room. They were receiving letters daily from fans all
over the world. Most of them came from little girls, who were
inspired by Dorothy's heroism.

Other locals from Chinatown were lining up to fill the
printing press positions. There was only one item missing to
finish their new location off: a proper street sign. It would have
to compete with their neighbor's infamous lit-up awning for the
Shanghai Low club.

Uncle Shu had been working on the sign while
Dorothy was setting up the office space. He kept the sign a
secret. It was covered with canvas. Dorothy watched as her
uncle went in and out from under the canvas to the bamboo
scaffolding right outside the office windows.

On the day of the grand opening. Dorothy, her Mom
and Dad, and Uncle Shu stood outside on the street. A long
rope was attached to the canvas still covering the sign. Uncle
looked at Dorothy and handed her the rope.

"Are you ready to unveil the new magazine?"

"Yes!" she shouted as she gave the rope a hard tug. The canvas over the sign slid off the front and to the ground. Dorothy was left staring up in disbelief at what she saw.

It read "Dorothy Summer's Monster Magazine".

Dorothy looked at Uncle after admiring the sign as it lit up the street in the dusk sky.

"Uncle are you sure about this?"

Uncle grabbed Dorothy's hand endearingly. "I am always sure. It wasn't Wang Shu whose stories made the *Monster Magazine* world famous. That was Dorothy Summers. One of the bravest women I have ever come to know."

"But this was your business. You started it."

"Ah yes, but like with everything, there comes a time for an end. My time has ended, and now I'm passing the torch over to you."

"Does that mean you aren't going to write for the magazine anymore?"

"Write? No. Help out? Yes. Someone has to keep watch over the magazine, while you're away chasing the next monster story."

Uncle's statement was both sweet, reassuring, and dooming at the same time. He brought up one point that Dorothy had not thought of realistically. The first story came to her by chance in the mail at the *Chronicle*. The question now stood: where would she find the next one?

A LETTER FROM NEW DELHI

Issue 21

A month had passed since the grand opening of *Dorothy Summer's Monster Magazine*. Dorothy, who was stir crazy from being in the office too long, was studying over some old articles of Wang Shu's. She was interrupted by her mother, who had left her post in the mail room.

In her mother's hand was an opened envelope and some folder parchment. Hanging out the edges of the parchment was a small piece of torn burgundy cloth.

"I think I found a letter you might find important.", her mother stated.

Dorothy reached to grab the papers out of her Mother's hand. Once she had them in her grasp, her eye was drawn straight to the burgundy cloth. She opened the papers to reveal the cloth inside. It was the same type of cloth that the story of the *Mystery of the Blue Dragon* had been written on. The one she had found under a pile of letters all the way back at the *Chronicle*.

Dorothy held the cloth in her left hand as she opened the pages of the letter in her right to read them. She asked her Mom to go get Uncle as she read the contents of the letter.

"*Dorothy,*

Now I know the name of the one who received my letter many months ago. From what I have read, you already know my name, Lhami. I found your story when I took a trip to the market in New Delhi.

I was pleased to read that the Blue Dragon of China was saved. After escaping the Tongs at the monastery, I went to Shanghai. While there, I took my robe and tore it into a hundred pieces. I wrote my letter on every piece, requesting help from anyone who would listen. I then sent the pieces out to newspapers all over the world.

I would have never guessed that the Universe would choose you to answer my call. I give thanks that it did.

The Blue Dragon might yet survive due to your efforts. Though there is not cause for full celebration.

*Your actions to save that life has caused a ripple effect
in the world. The story of the dragon has reached all
ears, both good and evil.*

*I fear there are some in the British Empire here in
New Delhi that wish to seek out the guardian of the
mother creatures. Their intentions with the
knowledge the guardian holds do not seem to be
honorable.*

*I must ask you for help once more. Help us to protect
the secrets of the Guardian.*

Brother Monk - Lhami."

At the bottom of the page was a pressed seal indented
into the parchment. It looked like a Tapuat symbol, but
different in a way. As Dorothy was rubbing her fingers across
the symbol, her uncle came into her office.

"Your mother said you called for me." Uncle paused
before looking at the letter in Dorothy's hand. "What is that
you have there?"

"Our next story."

Humanity. A species originated on planet Earth. We hold the capability to transform the Universe of our dimension around us. Our limits are far reaching. Greatness lies within us all yet is unlocked through shear will from only a few. The greatness that the powerful among us unleash, is that of both destruction and creation. Throughout time our nature yields to progression. Never perfect, but always improving. The efforts do not belong to any single ideology. All known divisions of our species have created and destroyed. The common thread: our individuality's purpose in the whole. Our race, gender, sexuality, age, or genetics. These are physical traits that hold no value but split our species amongst invisible lines. What value do we hold? How do we define who we are? We belong to humanity. We are individuals. Ever-changing, like our own species. We are defined by our choices, our ideas. We mold them towards progression. The only similarity between us all, is the red blood in our veins. There is a push to rise above our biological identities, and to ascend into enlightenment. These are my stories; my identity is stitched within. I change with every word, every page, and every second. I am no longer what you read but progressing with my fellow humans. Reaching out to a better tomorrow. I am the REDWRITER.

Made in the USA
Monee, IL
01 November 2020